Pretenders

The Hellénus Cato Affair

Pretenders

The Hellénus Cato Affair

A Novel by

Fernand Hibbert

Translated by Matthew Robertshaw

Deux Voiliers Publishing

First Edition 2018

English translation copyright © Matthew Robertshaw

ISBN 978-1-928049-50-0

Translation of original work by Fernand Hibbert published in French as *Les Simulacres*, 1923.

Published in Canada by

Deux Voiliers Publishing, Aylmer, Quebec.

www.deuxvoilierspublishing.com

Cover Art – Matthew Robertshaw

Cover Design – Ian Thomas Shaw

To Simone André Vieux. – F.H.

To Jack James Norman Robertshaw. – M.R.

When Fernand Hibbert penned his final novel, *Les Simulacres*, his native Haiti had been occupied by the United States for eight years. When the Marines first landed in Port-au-Prince in 1915, and the U.S. government subsequently took the reins of the Haitian administration, many Haitians were hopeful that it would be an opportunity to finally achieve the stability and development that had long eluded the Caribbean nation. The Americans, for their part, claimed they would bring democracy and economic progress to Haiti. But by the 1920s, whether because of the violent tactics used against Caco resistance fighters like Charlemagne Peralte, the occupiers' recourse to forced labour reminiscent of slavery for public works projects, the pervasive racism evinced by Marines from the Jim Crow South, or simply the fact that their country seemed to have lost its hard-won independence, Haitians at all levels of society began to become disillusioned with the Occupation. This is the backdrop of Hibbert's final novel.

The story revolves around a love affair between Céphise Cato and a foreigner, the Cuban Pablo Alcantara y Toro, with Céphise's husband Hellénus standing by as the hapless cuckold. The trio comes across as a powerful indictment of the pretensions underpinning the Occupation; the Haitian people are made impotent by the invading foreigners who take liberties with their homeland. But Hibbert's Pretenders, his Simulacra, are not only those foreigners who presume to infringe upon Haitian sovereignty; the author is more famous as a critic of his own class, the Haitian bourgeoisie, as seen in his earlier novels. *Pretenders* is no exception. Here Hibbert also takes aim at his compatriots who, by their indefatigable intrigues, allowed the Occupation to come about in the first place. In his final refrains, Hibbert calls for the Haitian people to pull themselves up by their bootstraps. "All we have before us are the Simulacra," he says, "and it is only a matter of preparing ourselves to make them withdraw and disappear—and to stop being Simulacra ourselves." In sum, his message is a warning against exploitation from foreign powers as well as from self-interested local elites.

Hibbert's message is as pertinent today as it was when the novel appeared in 1923. Today, as much as ever, Haitian sovereignty is subordinated to foreign interests, as Robert Fatton Jr. has explored in his 2013 study *Haiti: Trapped in the Outer Periphery*. Likewise, indigenous Simulacra continue to plague the nation. As I write this introduction, in December of 2018, Haiti is once again in a state of turmoil, as thousands have joined in anti-corruption protests against the Haitian government's mishandling of billions of dollars meant for reconstruction after the 2010 earthquake. But although Hibbert's Simulacra survive nearly a century later, so too does his message, embodied in those who will not stand by and impotently allow Pretenders to have their way with their country. If there are still Pablo Alcantaras, the Hellénus Catos are becoming fewer and fewer.

Matthew Robertshaw, December 2018

CHAPTER I

HELLÉNUS CATO, HAVING attended Mass at "The Sisters" of Lalue, was heading back up the avenue of the same name, breathing the fresh morning air.

His wife and three of her lady friends followed close behind; they were struggling to make conversation, for want of material. The few monosyllables that made it to Mr. Hellénus Cato's ears told him that the ladies were preoccupied with the supposed marriage prospects of some recent widowers who, whether they had been happy or unhappy the first time, seemed to be uninterested in resuming conjugal life.

Other groups of ladies, on exiting the chapel and heading up or down the avenue, were also discussing hypothetical matches.

Suddenly, Mr. Hellénus Cato stopped and shouted:

"Good day, *Maître*!"

This sign of attention was addressed to a man in pyjamas who, sitting at the edge of his garden, was reading a book and separating its pages as he went.

Mr. Brion—such was his name—looked up and politely responded to his neighbour's greeting.

Then Mr. Hellénus Cato turned back to his wife and cried:

"Céphise, go on home without me. I'm going to swap a few ideas with our neighbour."

Hearing this, Mr. Brion closed the book, carefully placing the paper cutter in the book where he had left off. Then he got up and walked over to his morning visitor. They shook hands and went together back to the section of the garden that Mr. Brion had just left.

Taking their seats, Mr. Hellénus Cato condescendingly blurted out:

"Always with those books!"

Mr. Brion smiled sweetly:

"Always," he replied.

"How do you get on?"

"I don't know. But books offer me subjects for meditations and daydreams. This lets me stand out and helps me to keep on living."

"Really!"

And after a short silence, Mr. Hellénus Cato added:

"Personally, as soon as I start reading, I fall asleep."

Mr. Brion considered this kind-heartedly and said:

"You seem to speak the truth."

And the silence resumed.

Mr. Hellénus Cato was a man of about fifty-eight years, though he looked younger. He had helped to establish of one of those former governments that did not last long, but that benefited the "eligible parties," as they used to say. He was named a minister, he persecuted his compatriots, committed a few crimes, and after a year at the Ministry, which he had entered as a beggar, he accumulated a small fortune which he managed to keep—a rare occurrence among politicians of that type. The American intervention derailed his ascension, "destroyed his prospects," as he sometimes grumbled. Regrets buried his soul; he became an ardent patriot and a bitter progressive.

He loved chatting with Mr. Brion whom he knew to be a free spirit and an *honnête homme*. And that Sunday Mr. Hellénus Cato was particularly disposed to "spew invective," to cite an expression that he often used.

Mr. Brion continued to keep his silence, weary, no doubt, of his neighbour's visits and rants. Anyway, what wasn't he weary of? This grey-haired, fresh-faced and deeply sensitive man had never fully recovered from a broken heart he had suffered in his youth. Just like René's father, he "yawned through life"—and, it seemed to him, with better reason—and found some distraction in human folly, or more specifically Haitian folly.

Mr. Hellénus Cato, keeping an eye on his friend, looked for a way to steer the conversation toward what he really wanted to talk about: the government and the Americans. As for Brion, forgetting the presence of his visitor, he had allowed his thoughts to wander back to the book he held in his hands, which was a volume of new biographical and bibliographic research on Stendhal.

"Where," he asked himself, "where does this attraction to Stendhal come from? His words have stirred my soul since my youth. The man, as much as his works, has never ceased to interest me.

"I often reread Phèdre, Andromaque, Bérénice, Britannicus, but what do I care about the man in Racine's works, the things he has done, the words he said? Whereas the smallest excerpt of Stendhal stops me in my tracks. He wrote things that, before him, no one had dared to admit: "My father died yesterday. He didn't love me. I didn't love him either," or this: "For me, Love was always the greatest pursuit, nay, the only." And this observation on a trip abroad: "Meeting a compatriot to me is death." Stendhal is the man who sees things as they really are—as opposed to the Simulacra, the lies behind which men mask the truth regarding their interests and appetites."

At that moment, Mr. Hellénus Cato shouted:

"Don't you see the problem?"

Mr. Brion returned to reality and levelled an expectant glance at his visitor.

"I no longer have a homeland!" Mr. Hellénus Cato yelled.

Mr. Brion smiled and said calmly:

"Everyone has a homeland."

But the other would hear none of it, and kept yelling:

"Traitors sold my country and handed it over to foreigners."

Mr. Brion stopped smiling.

"You know quite well," he said, "that no one has ever sold or handed the country over to anyone. The Americans came here of their own will, and when they debarked in

Port-au-Prince, after the massacres of July 1915, they found no central government or even a municipal authority."

"But there were the Chambers!"

"Yes, but they hadn't been elected by the nation; they were thus Simulacra. We appeared to have institutions and countless laws, but behind all that there were none of the realities that distinguish a civilized nation: no principles, no control, no political parties to condition and guarantee peace, order and liberty, and no hopes for such developments. No sir, when the Americans set foot in Haiti, they didn't encounter men who sold or handed them anything, they only encountered Lies and Insincerity. And they had no trouble cutting through those clouds. Many Haitians, therefore, saw the Occupation as a positive thing."

"I'm not saying," said Mr. Hellénus Cato, calming himself, "I'm not discussing those points. It's just that those men have no right to monopolize our country and do whatever they want."

"They started off by giving us peace and order," continued Mr. Brion, ignoring Mr. Cato's interruption. "We now have freedom of expression and other liberties will follow. The development of the country by work and commerce is imminent (particularly since the Americans have a stake in it, since they hold our entire public debt), but it all depends on the organization of universal primary education. Progress is impossible if the people are unable to read or write, and in our case they don't even have the rudiments."

"The way I see it," said Mr. Cato, "the main problem is political. They should let us handle our own affairs and start by pissing off."

"The question of universal primary education," Mr. Brion continued, "is of the highest importance. It will cost a lot of money. The help and the collaboration of the Americans will be indispensable. In the United States, education is admirably organized. Still, I wonder whether it would suit us better, in our particular case, to follow the model that Lunacharsky has just set up in Russia."

"What the hell is a Lunacharsky?"

"He's Lenin's Minister of Education."

"What has he done?"

"Besides the obligatory school attendance of children aged eight to thirteen—complete with food, clothes and school supplies paid for by the State—where the curriculum is general, there is a second cycle from thirteen to sixteen in which the students are prepared for working life in their country by giving them experience with the principal branches of production. The essential idea in both cycles is to mould each child not just into a citizen, but into a productive citizen. Anyhow, all this has yet to be discussed. When I said that it would suit us better to follow Lunacharsky's model, I was mostly referring to what in Russia is called the liquidation of ignorance, which is to say, the attempt to educate ignorant adults. Morizet's chapter on this subject should be consulted—and notice that Morizet took the trouble of going to see what was happening in Russia."

Here, Mr. Brion got up, crossed the veranda, disappeared into his study and soon returned with a little volume which he rifled through as he returned to Mr. Cato. Suddenly, he stopped and read the following aloud:

"Teaching children is merely fulfilling the duty of any government worthy of the name. To repair, in the generations beyond school age, a bit of the crime committed against them by the regime that previously ignored this duty is to understand the responsibility of a leader in the deepest sense of the word."

Mr. Brion closed the book and added:

"The government decreed that all residents from the age of eight to fifty who can't read or write were expected to learn to do so, and action was taken against those who tried to escape the decree's stipulations, or who prevented illiterates from attending school. And to prepare the necessary personnel to teach illiterate adults, courses were created. The decree is from 1919. One year later, the Commissariat of Education estimated that over the course of 1920 two million seven hundred thousand illiterates had learned the basic elements. And it continues."

He was silent for a moment and then said:

"Isn't that an example to imitate?"

"Certainly . . . certainly," said Mr. Hellénus Cato, "but we can and must accomplish such work on our own."

Mr. Brion smiled.

"You are well aware," he said, "that we can't accomplish such an undertaking on our own. Oh, when it comes to composing, copying or transposing laws, decrees, declarations, proclamations, we don't need a soul—we are master scribes. As soon as we've created a law, we think we've acted. But in such an activity as I've described, it's the execution, the results, that matter—and that hardly corresponds with our well-known system, for which the formula is: you must seem to do something. Again, it's the Simulacrum—but the Simulacrum in a more Byzantine form."

Mr. Hellénus Cato couldn't prevent himself from smiling on hearing these words; then becoming stern again, he exclaimed: "First of all, the Americans will never consent to help us in the undertaking of public education. They want our death, no more, no less."

"You think so?" said Mr. Brion, lighting a cigarette.

"I know so," replied Mr. Cato, who lit a native cigar, a *papouloute*.

"Well then, my dear Hellénus, I don't at all see things your way. I even believe—and this may scandalize you, so I ask your pardon in advance—I believe that the American wishes us well. Except, since he doesn't explain what he's doing, and he doesn't admit when he's wrong and knows it *in petto*, we tend to imagine the most crooked things about this taciturn and sullen tutor. Generally, it's not until long after he's acted that we understand what he was trying to do; and personally, I've never seen the observed act done with the intention of hurting us."

"Personally," said Mr. Cato excitedly, "I've always observed the opposite."

"Because you are biased. As a Minister under the old regime, you made a fortune . . ."

"Not at all!" Mr. Cato protested with indignation. "I didn't make a centime when I was in office. That's a bloody slander, and I'm shocked to hear you repeat it, you, whom I consider a friend! I was a patriot, I am a patriot, I will always be a patriot!"

Mr. Hellénus Cato had not always been the resolute man that he claimed to be. Mr. Brion could recall a time, not long before—it was shortly after Port-au-Prince had hosted the fine, elegant and sophisticated Senator Medill McCormick who had recommended that the Occupation have more contact with Haitian society. One day, Mrs. Russell, along with Mrs. Henry Roberts, had come to visit Mrs. Céphise Cato. Hellénus was so proud that he spent two full days puffed up like a balloon. Céphise too. Just think! Mrs. Roberts's visit alone would have been enough to flatter her—and there was the wife of the head of the Occupation tagging along to see her, extending invitations; she was overwhelmed! Mrs. Roberts, who had never met the Catos, made the introductions with admirable grace. Mrs. Russell found Céphise lovely, feisty, which she was; and although Hellénus's solemnity almost made her laugh, she knew better, congratulated him on being the husband of such a charming woman, and then she left with her friend.

That was all, but it was enough. What perspective future this little visit instilled in Mr. Cato's soul, one can only guess! The next week, Céphise paid back the visit, accompanied by her husband. They also went to see Mr. and Mrs. Roberts. Within a few weeks, Mr. Hellénus Cato had turned into an Americanizing-Americanist, and stopped, for a time, seeing Mr. Brion. But when he realized that the Americans were not planning to make him president of the Republic, he slowly began to deflate, reverted to patriotism and resumed visiting Mr. Brion, who welcomed him with his smile, full of goodwill and sweet irony.

But let us return to the conversation that we had to interrupt to give this background information.

"I was a patriot, I am a patriot, I will always be a patriot!" Mr. Hellénus Cato had exclaimed.

"It was never my intention to offend you, my dear Hellénus," said Mr. Brion. "In bringing up your ascent to the Ministry in the good old days and saying that you didn't neglect your own interests, I only meant to pay homage to you. As for your patriotism, I respect that."

"I thank you, *Maître*, for your kind words and, despite everything, I feel the greatest esteem for you. What irks me is your insistence on defending the Americans, you, their victim, because you abandoned a permanent post in order to enter the Ministry where you were unable to sustain yourself."

"But I'm not defending them. I'm trying to understand them, that's all. Besides, I wasn't their victim for not having stayed at the Ministry. I left willingly. My law practice is sufficiently, if not completely, satisfying."

"Maybe so. But you lost your job security."

"I lost my security in the Appeals Court, but I'm secure in my profession, and I prefer it that way."

Mr. Hellénus Cato was about to reply when he was approached by his servant, Bernadotte, who had the ability to make the Lalue neighbourhood tremble single-handedly, even if cars were idling.

Bernadotte let his master know that Madame was waiting for him for breakfast.

Mr. Cato pulled out his watch.

"Damn! Eight o'clock!" he exclaimed. "Tell Madame I'm on my way."

Mr. Cato extended his hand to Mr. Brion.

"Goodbye, *Maître*."

"Goodbye, Hellénus."

"Say, sir," said Mr. Cato without releasing Mr. Brion's hand, "lend me your book on Russia."

Mr. Cato had great admiration for Bolshevism. Stripping an aristocracy of its wealth to benefit the people seemed to him the epitome of justice and of a policy worthy of the name. And he dreamed of a similar path for Haiti, which would profit him greatly. This strange communist, owner of many houses, storehouses and villas, intended to hold onto what he had and augment the number of his properties, because, for whatever reason, he considered himself 'a man of the people.' He did not imagine for a second that if somehow an upheaval were to take place in Haiti he would be among the aristocrats.

"My dear Hellénus, I'm very sorry, but I'm unable to fulfil your request. Ever since a book I lent to a friend was returned—after much trouble, mind you—with fifteen pages missing, I've vowed that no book is to be removed from my library by a compatriot."

"It pains me deeply," said Hellénus, his feelings hurt, "to be exposed to this refusal."

"It pains me even more deeply to be unable to comply. And when you consider that it's in virtue of a principle that I've acted thus, it's impossible that you, a man of principles, will fail to forgive me."

Mr. Hellénus Cato deigned to smile and, with a nod of his head, confirmed his satisfaction with these words, which touched his pretensions.

And Mr. Brion placed his hand on his friend's shoulder and accompanied him to the end of his driveway, and then they parted ways.

CHAPTER II

EVERY AFTERNOON, CÉPHISE Cato would sit in front of the gate leading to her villa, apparently thrilled to observe the hustle and bustle in the road. She was a lovely brunette with lively eyes, frizzy hair, and with plump, fleshy lips. When she laughed—which was often—one could see all of her teeth, which were brilliantly white, and two dimples sketched onto the corners of her mouth. Her nose, it must be said, was knavish, and a black spot at the base of her right cheek gave a certain *je ne sais quoi* to her already striking appearance. It was a joy to see her out walking or more precisely ambling about. Her whole lovely body moved. Accordingly, every day from five to seven, all the men would tip their hats to her as she ascended Lalue, whether by car, bus or buggy, whether on horseback or on foot.

When Mr. Hellénus Cato accompanied her, he naively believed that all these greetings were the palpable indication of his own popularity.

Céphise was thirty and looked twenty-two. She had never had children, and, despite her seductive charms, she was clever. Incidentally, Mr. Hellénus Cato never took her anywhere and never received guests, not so much because he was jealous, but because he had convinced himself that the Americans feared him and had surrounded him with a great network of detectives. Thus, you understand, he took precautions. He only went out for funerals. That was his way of cultivating his 'candidature.' As soon as he heard of someone's death, he would put on his double-breasted frock coat, which made him look immense—he was a handsome man, this Hellénus Cato—and don his bowler hat. Then, with his gloves clutched in his left hand as if he was afraid of them being stolen, and his ivory cane under his right arm, he could be seen standing near the arch at the front gate of his villa, awaiting the arrival of the buggy driven by Bernadotte, transformed into a coachman for the occasion.

He sometimes went out in the morning, around four o'clock, shabbily dressed, for walks of varying lengths, depending on his health.

As has been noted, on Sundays he would go to the six o'clock Mass with his wife.

Mr. Hellénus Cato, though not rich, was quite comfortable. He spent most of his time, just like everyone else, violently criticizing the government for what they were or were not doing. When he kept his silence, it was to think of ways to rid the nation of the Americans and get his revenge on his compatriots who thought differently or did not appreciate him as he desired. He only interrupted himself from time to time to yell at Bernadotte who was indifferent.

All in all, with a bit of philosophy, this man could have had a happy life, by giving a bit of joy to so many people suffering from hunger and a bit of relief to those unfortunates succumbing hopelessly under the weight of disease. But he preferred to hoard his possessions and to remain deplorably unhappy.

And yet he could be seen at the church, humble, repentant, contrite, addressing fervent prayers to God, who is goodness, tenderness and charity—to God, whose heart is so full of love for mankind that He poured out his blood for them, *et cetera*.

And he would then leave the chapel with nothing but hate in his heart.

In truth, he must not have understood—or perhaps the Simulacra are stronger than anything.

One afternoon, Mr. Hellénus Cato had just joined his wife near the gate to their villa, when an Overland automobile stopped across the road in front of Mr. Brion's porch. A handsome young man stepped out, waved to the Catos, and headed up the lawyer's driveway.

"Who is that man?" Mr. Hellénus Cato asked.

"He's a foreigner," Céphise replied. "I don't know his name."

"The last two Sundays he has sat near us at Mass," said Mr. Cato, "and he didn't take his eyes off of us."

"I didn't notice," said Céphise, who most certainly had been aware of the foreigner's interest.

"He must be some spy for the Americans."

"I don't know. Surely Mr. Brion can tell you about him."

"There's an idea."

After the foreigner left, Mr. Hellénus Cato crossed the road and approached Mr. Brion, whom he found examining the roses in his garden.

"Ah ha!" Mr. Cato exclaimed. "When you're not with your books, you're with your flowers."

"You're more fortunate than I am, my dear Hellénus, since you have the happiness of enjoying the company of a woman whom you love and who loves you, which is preferable to the company of roses and books."

"Well then, why don't you get married?"

"I was unable to when I was young. Now that I'm almost fifty it's too late . . ."

"It's never too late to do a good thing," Mr. Cato said sententiously. "At forty-eight, I married a young girl of twenty, and have been happy for ten years."

"The gods have spoiled you, Hellénus, and I don't have your luck. In any case, if circumstances find me in the presence of a woman whom I love and who loves me, I promise to do likewise."

"I'll hold you to that."

A silence fell. Mr. Cato broke it with an assault on the government, and the recent nomination of another corrupt man to a public post.

Mr. Brion, amused by this, smiled, and let him ramble on.

When Mr. Cato had finished unburdening himself, he breathed with satisfaction and said:

"So, who was that whippersnapper with you a minute ago?"

"He's a client who came for a consultation on some legal points. It's the second time he's come here. I don't know why he doesn't come to my office in town."

"He's a foreigner, a Cuban perhaps?"

"Yes. He told me he lived in France for many years, and in Puerto Rico. He seems more Italian than Cuban. I found him very intelligent. I have his business card here. His name is Pablo Alcantara."

"What's he doing here?"

"He's trying to get established. He has heaps of projects. You would like him a lot, as he hates the government and abhors Americans."

"He's a good man, then."

"If you say so!"

"As long as he's not an undercover agent of the Americans," said Mr. Cato, becoming suspicious again.

"To what end? The Americans, who are cleverer than you think, wouldn't waste their time paying a detective to survey a man like me who never conspired under the old regime. They're only interested in former professional conspirators, and almost all of those are enrolled in the ranks of informers in their security service, which is fine by me. No, Mr. Alcantara's dissatisfaction is real and springs from the government's rejection of one of his projects, which the Americans mocked."

"Does this character at least pay you for these consultations?" asked Mr. Cato.

"On the spot. His wallet is bursting with greenbacks."

"Ah!"

This last comment added to the effect of the Overland, giving Mr. Alcantara great prestige Mr. Cato's eyes.

However, this foreigner did seem more than suspect to Mr. Brion. Besides the fact that the rogue in him was evident at every moment—which Mr. Brion could not mention, he was a client after all—there was also the way he would come for consultation at Mr. Brion's private home instead of his office in the heart of the city, where Alcantara spent his days. The subject of his consultations was not even anything serious and seemed more like a pretext to approach the lawyer, for who knows what reason, all this piqued Mr. Brion's interest wonder, since he liked to see things and people clearly.

He was not troubled—nothing ever troubled him— nevertheless, he was intrigued.

As for Mr. Hellénus Cato, not being able to learn anything else about Alcantara, he soon left.

Mr. Brion, left alone in the driveway, seemed to reflect for a moment. Then, glancing over at the house across the road, he saw Mr. Hellénus Cato who, with lively gestures, was obviously relating their conversation to his wife. Céphise listened, breathless.

And so, a glimmer crossed Mr. Brion's mind, and he decided he would get to the bottom of the true motive behind the frequent consultations of Mr. Pablo Alcantara y Toro.

CHAPTER III

Two days later, around five o'clock in the evening, Mr. Brion was sitting under his veranda (which in Haiti is called a *galerie*) with one of his friends, Mr. Renaudin, an enlightened Haitian merchant, when Mr. Pablo Alcantara arrived bearing a small, carefully packaged box. Mr. Brion welcomed him with his usual courtesy and introduced him to Mr. Renaudin.

"Sorry to bother you," said the newcomer, turning toward Mr. Brion, "I am not here for a consultation today, I am just bringing you this box of high-quality Havana cigars, which I just received and which I ask you to accept as a token of my gratitude, my friendship and my admiration."

Mr. Brion replied that he did not believe he deserved all these compliments and honours; that as a general rule he didn't accept gifts from anyone; that he, however, thanked Mr. Alcantara for his present which he accepted, not wanting to offend a foreigner; but that in the future, he asked him to refrain.

Mr. Alcantara was sincerely astonished by this speech because, since he had been in Haiti, everyone would ask him for boxes of cigars from his country. He did not mention any of this, but merely understood from it that Mr. Brion was one-of-a-kind.

Mr. Brion invited Mr. Alcantara to sit with them and noticed that the Cuban positioned his chair so that he could see, and be seen by, Céphise, from where she was sitting in front of the gate to her villa.

"Well then," thought Mr. Brion, "the secret in the conduct of Don Pablo is no longer a mystery to me, it's love . . . and no ordinary love, judging by the way he's blushing and casting fiery glances at the Lady of his thoughts."

Mr. Brion had seen correctly. Pablo Alcantara had noticed Céphise on his third day in Port-au-Prince, and it had been love at first sight. Men of his race do not know how to half-love; for them, love immediately erupts into a furious passion. It was as if Pablo was possessed. And the impossibilities he faced in approaching this beauty—Mr. Cato never received visitors for any reason—consumed him completely. He thus decided on an indirect course, which is to say, to start an association with Mr. Brion in order to gain the trust of Mr. Hellénus Cato, about whom he had learned incredible things. To overpower the latter, to persuade him to invite him to his home, to make Céphise fall in love with him, to convince her to divorce her husband and marry him straightaway—all this was child's play for Pablo who failed to consider the Simulacra, who live in the shadows.

Not five minutes after Mr. Pablo Alcantara sat down in the company of Mr. Brion and Mr. Renaudin, Mr. Hellénus Cato, informed, no doubt by Céphise, of the presence of the foreigner at Mr. Brion's home, went over to join the group. Mr. Cato already knew Mr. Renaudin; Mr. Brion introduced him to Pablo. The two men shook hands profusely and exchanged exaggerated compliments. Then they both took a seat.

After a short silence, the conversation started rolling. Mr. Cato began naturally with a heated attack against the Government, which is to say the President of the Republic —since he is the Government. Mr. Renaudin and Mr. Cato were having a field day. Pablo showed his support with looks and smiles, constantly chortling heartily. Mr. Brion contented himself with laughing.

Was he laughing at his guests or at the Government? Maybe at the lot of them—life was such a spectacle for him.

"I notice, Brion, that you tend to spare the Government," said Mr. Renaudin, who, however, had never cared much for politics. "Why is that?"

"Because I don't think it's fair to attack a Government that doesn't operate freely," Mr. Brion replied calmly.

"If it operated freely, this Government would persecute all those who didn't grovel before it," Mr. Renaudin retorted.

"Then you approve of the American who restrains the Government and the people, judging apparently that both must have an apprenticeship in liberty?"

"It seems to me," said Mr. Renaudin, "that the American has put no restraints on the Government, since the latter voted on press censorship, which you surely don't approve of, Brion, as it is a law that limits liberty."

"And unconstitutional!" Mr. Hellénus Cato exclaimed.

"Indeed, I don't approve of it," said Mr. Brion. "No one approves of it. It's one of those laws made in a fit of nervous haste. And like all emergency laws, it will disappear at the first opportunity. Furthermore, I think a Head of State should be able to suffer injury. Hence my admiration for Pericles, Caesar, Frederick II King of Prussia, Alexandre Pétion and Boisrond-Canal. They were Heads of State with all the means to take revenge on their critics, and yet disdained to do it."

"You forgot Vespasian," said Mr. Renaudin.

"No, I didn't forget him," replied Mr. Brion. "In my mind, Vespasian's fame is forever soiled by his having put to death Thrasea's son-in-law, Helvidius Priscus, senator and stoic philosopher, who had adamantly opposed him."

And Mr. Brion added:

"Helvidius Priscus, the indomitable spirit. Mr. Louis-Edouard Pouget is the spitting image of him."

"In any case," Mr. Hellénus Cato exclaimed, "Mr. Pouget is luckier than Helvidius Priscus, he hasn't been killed!"

Mr. Brion looked Mr. Hellénus Cato straight in the eyes and said:

"Liberty is more precious than life."

Then Mr. Renaudin brought the discussion back to the Americans whom he held responsible for the law on press censorship, and he asked Mr. Brion to explain why two directors of nationalist newspapers had been arrested while their contributors, who were clearly more violent than the directors, were left alone.

"How am I to explain what I don't understand?" Mr. Brion replied.

Still, the discussion grew more impassioned. Mr. Brion's moderation frustrated Messrs. Renaudin and Cato. Mr. Brion, who loved truth as much as liberty, tried to regulate the conversation by seeking to reconcile contradictions, according to his custom.

"I notice," Mr. Cato cried, "that Mr. Brion goes even easier on the Americans than he does the Government."

"You forget, my dear Hellénus, that I was Secretary of State under the regime of the Convention, and by consequence, I permitted the regime. I am therefore interested in the way in which American actions in Haiti will lead to positive results for us."

"But that's impossible!" Mr. Renaudin and Mr. Hellénus Cato shouted.

"Why?"

"Those men hate the country and have coldly condemned it to degradation and death, it's obvious!" Mr. Renaudin cried with hate in his eyes.

"And only their accomplices don't see it!" Mr. Cato yelled furiously, beside himself.

"Listen, Hellénus," Mr. Brion said dryly, "I want you to tell me what accomplices you're talking about."

Mr. Cato explained that when he was referring to certain undesirable 'brigands.' And he cited a few of his personal enemies.

"*Maître*," he added in a pained tone, "how could you imagine, you whom I love so much, that a malicious thought about you would cross my mind?"

"It is forgotten," said Mr. Brion.

And to think, he said to himself, this is the public opinion. And if the current system, as bad as it is, is not modified, the lack of co-operation will bring destruction.

"Well!" Mr. Renaudin cried. "Those people hate us so much that they won't even consult with us! We have to accept their projects exactly as they are, without being able to change them one iota!"

Mr. Brion replied:

"I don't believe they act that way because they hate us, it's more likely because of distrust since they distrust us as much as we distrust them. As Bailly-Blanchard said, 'There are about thirty types of tricksters and cheats who are always ready to set another project against the one you present, and to demolish the plan in a heartbeat by changing a single word! . . .' It seems to me that those people, to speak like Renaudin, know us well and assess us rather correctly."

"Ah! Bailly-Blanchard said that," said Mr. Renaudin, whose national pride was flattered—not seeing the criticism that the opinion implied, that is to say, discussion for the sake of discussion, change for the sake of change, and that such a character, like Thomas Diafoirus, was always ready to support the 'contrary proposition.'

"In any case," said Mr. Hellénus Cato, "these Americans have locked us into a vicious cycle, and I don't see how we can get out of it."

"We will get out of it by freedom of the press and freedom of speech," cried Mr. Brion. "The work of the *Union Patriotique* and the campaigns of nationalist newspapers will bear fruit. If only all those skilled writers would take up their pens and discuss the interests of their country. Let us show we are attentive to all the matters that concern us. After the emergency regime that has been imposed on us, which makes us cringe, there will come a political regime that will safeguard the dignity of the people. We must not get discouraged, we must, on the contrary, persevere. Things may improve faster if we decide to show respect to the citizen who has been honoured with the title of President of the Republic."

"And if he doesn't deserve our respect?" asked Mr. Renaudin.

"From the moment that he is Head of State, he has a right to our respect and our esteem," replied Mr. Brion. "He is the one who represents the Country—the only one! To insult him, to lift yourself up to the level of his prestige, is to diminish the nation itself."

"If we don't tell him the truth, he'll end up doing whatever he wants," Mr. Renaudin exclaimed in a rage.

"Tell him all the truth you want to, but without offending him," said Mr. Brion. "And the saddest part of all this is that you don't even see who is profiting from all these divisions! You don't even realize who has a stake in them."

"Personally," he added, "I believe that since his un-happy accession to Head of State in that Palace . . ."

"The 'White Mausoleum!'" Mr. Renaudin sneered.

Mr. Brion smiled at his friend's interruption and re-sumed:

"Well! I believe that since his unhappy accession, under the weight of Destiny, to the position of principal Host of the 'White Mausoleum', he is to be pitied rather than envied."

"Listen, my dear Brion," said Mr. Renaudin, "we are old friends, and since we've known each other we've never agreed on anything; and still, in the end you have been proved right, I understand that. And that can be explained. I am a man of passion and you've found a way never to become impassioned about anything."

"I'm a monster, no?"

"Time will tell," said Mr. Renaudin, who added: "I want you to tell me how treating the President with respect will in any way help with our problems."

"I think," Mr. Brion replied, "that a president who is accepted, respected and understood will take great prestige from this fact and will easily be able to justify the opinion with the appropriate actions. Obviously, discipline is needed on both sides. In any case, one thing is certain: the sooner we realize this, the sooner the Americans will start to take us seriously."

Mr. Renaudin did not accept Mr. Brion's point of view, which Mr. Hellénus Cato deemed an "ideology."

Mr. Brion did not mind the use of the term, which in Mr. Hellénus Cato's mind was synonymous with madness.

Pablo had long lost interest in the conversation. He had crossed his arms and seemed to have fallen into a deep meditation—which did not prevent him from casting a glance, every now and then, toward the road, as if to make sure his car was still safe. But Mr. Brion saw that at those moments, the Cuban and Céphise were making eyes at each other, as the common expression goes.

When the conversation ended after Mr. Cato uttered the word ideology, Mr. Brion had refreshments served to the gentlemen and offered them cigars and cigarettes.

The day was ending and the moon, for the first time that month, showed a thin and pale crescent against a cloudless sky. Mr. Hellénus Cato, after having lit a cigar, headed toward the driveway as if to stretch his legs, made sure no one was paying attention to him, crossed himself energetically and whispered a short prayer facing the dark orb, then he went back to his seat, blowing puffs of smoke toward the ceiling.

Mr. Hellénus Cato's little promenade was observed only by Pablo, for whom it was a ray of light.

I have it, thought the Cuban, who started talking, in an inspired tone, about life's abundant mysteries; the extraordinary things he had seen accomplished by Manès, the rich Spaniard, resident of Santa-Clara, Cuba, with the help of some simple calculations based on the observation of the planets and particularly the moon—'la loune,' as he pronounced the French *lune*!

"And what extraordinary things did you see this Manès accomplish?" Mr. Renaudin asked.

"Oh! Incredible things! Miracles! Actual miracles! He coured people of leprosy, or tuburcoulosis, rare diseases that were repoutedly the most incourable of all! I joined him on a trip to Spain, where the king had summoned him for a consultation. It was thanks to the results of his calcoulations that the king, enlightened about his whole fouture, avoided all the attempted assassinations that the anarchists plotted against his person. I went with him to Mexico, to Don Venoustiano Cerranza whom he helped find the famous treasure of the Aztecs—and if Don Venoustiano had listened to him, he would have avoided the treasonous death being prepared for him. But Don Venoustiano said, poor devil, that one cannot know the fouture of which only God possesses the secret. On the other hand, Menocal did listen to him, and thanks to Manès, he was re-elected President and he eluded all the bombs that were intended for him . . ."

"That really is wonderful!" Mr. Hellénus Cato exclaimed, in rapture.

"And he never resuscitated the dead, this Manès friend of yours?" asked Mr. Brion, imperturbably serious.

"Oh! Yes," said Pablo, without offering proof, "Oh! Yes . . . except that is even more difficult."

"Surely it's not any more difficult than the other miracles," said Mr. Brion.

"Oh! Yes, much more difficult!"

"Why?"

"Because," Pablo replied, "you have to base your calcoulations on the planet Neptoune, which can only be seen with a houge telescope."

"I see that you have an answer for everything," said Mr. Brion, forcing himself to maintain his seriousness.

Mr. Renaudin did not say anything; he thought that Pablo was duped by Manès, plain and simple.

As for Mr. Hellénus Cato, he was positively ecstatic in the presence of the Cuban. He, the politician whom no one had ever been able to cheat, was powerless in the domain of mystery and believed everything the man had said, and was prepared to swallow more, his credulity having no limits.

Pablo, now, was silent. He had crossed his arms again and was looking intently at the ceiling.

Mr. Hellénus Cato understood that the Cuban was communicating with Manès. Since Mr. Brion had information that Mr. Renaudin did not, he alone was amused.

Soon Mr. Brion's visitors left. Mr. Renaudin went first. Mr. Hellénus Cato soon followed; he left at the same time as Pablo, with whom he chatted for a long time in front of Mr. Brion's gate, beside the car.

CHAPTER IV

THE PREVIOUS NIGHT, JUST AS he parted ways with the Cuban, Mr. Hellénus Cato had done something unbelievable, disconcerting, and that was in opposition to his most irreducible principles: he had invited Mr. Pablo Alcantara to his house, for the following day around five o'clock in the afternoon.

At the appointed hour, the Cuban's car pulled into Mr. Hellénus Cato's driveway: the latter was waiting for his friend impatiently at the top of the steps of his villa, along with Mrs. Cato.

The Overland had arrived at the foot of the steps and had turned around to face the exit. Mr. Pablo Alcantara stepped out of his *maquina*—he never called it anything else—and quickly reached the platform where his hosts were standing.

"You are welcome in my home, Mr. Alcantara," said Mr. Hellénus Cato, who, after a pause, gestured to his wife and added:

"Madame Cato!"

"You are not unknown to me, Monsieur," Céphise said openly, "my husband talks about you all the time."

Pablo bowed and cautiously kissed the plump hand that was offered to him, muttering that Mr. Cato was too kind to his friends.

"No, no," Mr. Cato insisted with conviction. "You are an extraordinary man!"

"Spare me, I beg of you," said the other, blushing.

Pablo was led into the salon, which he found tastefully decorated. It had not always been so, but since Céphise had paid her visit to Mrs. Roberts, she had transformed her house following the Parisian style, which she had emulated down to the smallest detail.

Pablo was charmed by Céphise's grace and poise. She was a laureate of the Saint-Rose de Lima boarding school where she had grown accustomed to successfully playing the princess in dramas and the mischievous maidservant in comedies in the performances that accompanied the annual prize ceremonies.

"I find Mrs. Cato altogether charming," Pablo whispered into the ear of her husband.

"Yes, she's a first-rate woman," said Hellénus without modesty.

"And have you enjoyed Port-au-Prince?" Céphise asked with an engaging smile.

"Oh! Very much!"

"Have you seen some society people?"

"I can say that I have seen everyone, and Haitians are unimaginably welcoming."

"Indeed, Haitian loves foreigners."

"And you know, Madame, that is a virtue unique to your country. Anywhere else, the foreigner is thought of as an enemy."

"Here, conversely, Haitians think of other Haitians as enemies."

"Yes, I have noticed that you slander one another to no end. You feel no pride for your own. In Cuba, we honour our talented compatriots."

"Here, we exalt them on the day of their death, and then we never speak of them again."

"In Cuba, we enlarge them on their death, and we preserve their memory."

"Well, it's very good in your country, all my compliments, Monsieur!"

Mr. Hellénus Cato had held his tongue in order to let his wife shine. He judged, however, that it was time to interrupt, to put the conversation on the right path.

"I trust," he said, "that the Cuban government has dignity and that it has managed to bring the Americans into line."

Pablo did not dare admit that it was rather the Americans who had brought the Cuban government into line, and that, even under Menocal, when there was a certain stability, the said government published notes from the American government as if they were its own, without changing a word.

Given the situation, Pablo simply responded: "Certainly, certainly," and avoided speaking about things that were humiliating for his country, which is to say, for himself. And he commended Mrs. Cato for her exquisite taste in decorating the salon.

Céphise pouted:

"No, no . . . you're a flatterer, you know . . . it's the same as anywhere in Port-au-Prince."

"I assure you, Madame, that I am sincere in my judgement. Of the few salons I have seen in Port-au-Prince, yours is surely the most distinguished."

"Okay, I believe you," said Céphise, with feigned fatigue, never having doubted that her salon was one of the best in the capital.

Then they spoke about the drought, the dust that was accumulating everywhere. Bernadotte intervened right on time with a platter bearing three towering glasses full of chilled beer. They drank with satisfaction, as the weather was quite hot.

"I've noticed," said Céphise, "that you have a great fondness for our neighbour, Mr. Brion."

"Yes indeed!" Pablo replied, turning his eyes toward the floor. "He is quite transcendental!"

When a Cuban refers to someone as transcendental, they have said all they can say—it is the ultimate compliment.

"Does he visit you here sometimes?" Pablo asked.

"He never visits anyone," Mr. Cato replied, "except in special circumstances. His friends forgive him for this eccentricity and go see him all the same."

"He is a man who interests me greatly," Pablo resumed. "He exercises a real attraction on my soul, but I have not managed to discover anything specific about him. He is very intelligent, thinks for himself, knows about life, seems to have suffered much, and he is honest about it, kind, and full of good sense. When I speak of him, people only respond vaguely. Someone even dared to tell me he was a madman."

"I wouldn't think too much about that," said Céphise, laughing. "A madman, in Haiti, is anyone who doesn't agree with you! I've chatted with Mr. Brion many times. And, well! I have many delectable memories of those conversations. Everything he says to you causes pleasure; only you have to make him talk. It's rather curious."

"It does not surprise me," said Pablo.

"Personally," said Mr. Hellénus Cato, "although I don't agree with Mr. Brion about anything, I admire him. Unfortunately, he has a fatal flaw: he respects the Americans and our Government."

"Does he really respect them?" asked the Cuban. "My impression is that he sees Haitians as anarchic, and he uses the Americans as an example of the discipline that is necessary for your society. And you know, he is right. If you do not act in co-operation with your president, you are lost. This society, which is already deteriorating, will end up totally annihilating itself."

"I thought you were against the Government?"

"I was speaking in terms of ideas—my quarrel with your Government is beside the point."

Mr. Hellénus Cato seemed to reflect on these last words, while Céphise enjoyed Pablo's admiration; he threw her furtive glances almost incessantly.

The Cuban thought that he had overstayed his first visit and that it was time for him to go, but he could not bear to leave without telling his beloved about the passion that was devouring him.

And she, Céphise, with her mirthful face and gracious bearing, was more troubled than she let on. Her sentiments for her husband had changed over the last year: their conjugal love had become filial. And from time to time she let out a long sigh between two bursts of laughter. All told, she was unhappy! And as for the handsome man who desired her so passionately, she wanted him too. It was, in effect, the attraction of youth to youth! Was it her fault, the sensible Céphise, that Hellénus, despite his Herculean aspect, was only like Hercules in his bearing? Since after all, it must be noted that Hellénus, for some time, had been in the physical condition of the hero of the ditty "L'Af . . . P . . ." which the Count d'A. of S.S. diplomatically used to make clear his intentions, singing it for some lovely ladies of Turgeau and Peu-de-Chose who always asked him to recite it at the end of the merry dinners of our friend Lion.

Things being thus, it is easy to understand that Céphise also hoped to hear the words of love that Pablo was anxious to express to her.

But Mr. Hellénus Cato, who had finished reflecting on the observation Pablo had made about the need to co-operate with the Head of State, suddenly threw up his arms and said:

"Well then! No! We must never accept that man!"

"That is too bad," said the Cuban, getting up to leave.

He would rather leave without saying anything to his beloved than suffer another political conversation.

And he left heroically, promising to return the next day.

He did indeed return the following day, but Hellénus talked to him the whole time—not about politics this time—but about a man who interested him much more than politics, that being Manès, the Mage invented by Pablo in order to win the trust of Céphise's husband. For almost two hours the unfortunate man had to respond in specific details to all the questions that Mr. Hellénus Cato did not cease to ask him concerning Manès, the modern genie without equal.

Pablo left greatly dejected, not having been alone for a single second with Céphise, who seemed indifferent, but whose calm was, in fact, a paralyzing anxiety.

"Never," said the despairing lover to himself as he left, "never will I be able to say a word to my beloved while that man lives!"

And the Spanish blood that flowed in his veins churned continually. As he got into his *maquina*, he grumbled these unsettling words:

"One of us must vanish!"

However, forty-eight hours later he managed to talk to Céphise without having to kill anyone. The young woman was sitting, as she often did, in front of the gate to the villa, when Pablo came by. He parked the Overland near the archway and stepped out near Céphise who stood up. With a restrained ardour, without making any gestures, he immediately began expressing the emotions that had been smothering him for weeks. He stood straight, his hat in his hand. Passersby and neighbours could easily have believed that he was giving Mrs. Hellénus Cato a message for her husband.

Céphise listened to Pablo and stayed silent, but Pablo could see that she was not angry. She even invited him inside.

"My husband will be very unhappy when he learns that you came to greet me without consenting to pay him a little visit."

"No, no, that is impossible!" Pablo cried in terror.

Then he added, relatively calmly:

"I have accepted a dinner invitation for this evening at the home of some friends . . . I shall return tomorrow."

"Come a bit later. I'll be out the whole afternoon . . ."

"Very well, goodbye."

"Goodbye!"

"You let me leave like this, without a tender word . . ."

She smiled with emotion and tenderly pressed his hand as her only response.

He left as if drunk.

CHAPTER V

A FEW DAYS PASSED WITHOUT Mr. Brion seeing his visitor
Pablo, and Mr. Hellénus Cato seemed to be avoiding the
lawyer as the patriot had during his stint as an American-
ist.

One morning, when Mr. Brion was leaving his house
on his way to the office, he noticed Mr. Hellénus Cato
standing in the doorway of the *porte-cochère* of his villa.
The lawyer waved to him, then flagged down a bus. Mr.
Cato crossed the road, went over to him and started telling
him about the state of his health, which was greatly troubling his wife. It was an endless series of "I was saying to
my wife," and "my wife was saying to me." It seemed he
had been struck by every disease imaginable. Why all the
tall tales? He didn't know.

"And that is why, dear *Maître*, I haven't come to see
you recently. I am terribly sorry if you thought I'd become
indifferent."

"I was confident," Mr. Brion replied, "that you had important reasons to stay home. Otherwise, I wouldn't have been deprived of your amicable company."

"Anyway," Mr. Hellénus Cato continued, ashamed, "Mr. Alcantara has been coming regularly for short visits. He is so interesting!"

"Indeed."

"He's made the greatest impression on my wife."

"Even better then! Well," Mr. Brion added, "take care, and goodbye!"

"See you soon!" said Mr. Cato, who went back to his spot in front of the *porte-cochère*.

And Mr. Brion went to get onto the bus that was waiting for him when a car, coming down from Pétionville and driven by someone who needs no introduction, stopped near the bus, and Mr. Gerard Delhi yelled to Mr. Brion:

"Are you coming with me?"

"Gladly," said Mr. Brion.

The busman had become angry, but after Mr. Brion placed a 'consolation' in his hand, he regained his serenity!

"*Allons*, up!" said Mr. Delhi.

"Hold on," said Mr. Brion, inspecting his friend's car, "give me a chance to admire your beautiful *maquina*, as someone I know would say."

"It's a Dodge," Mr. Delhi replied, "but I'm only half happy with it; I'll only be satisfied when I get myself a Buick!"

"What! This craze has claimed you as well, eh?"

"My dear sir, you have no idea how much of a powerful diversion and a perfect anaesthetic the automobile is! It excuses you from acting, from thinking, from dreaming, from reading, from smoking, from eating, from making love. You drive, that's all. You drive the most breathless, the most fearful and the most submissive monster, which blasts down its paths cutting the air with fury—and you get all this just by placing your hands on the steering wheel, which, as someone said, has the mysterious and perfect shape of the Wheel of Fortune and Fate."

"You must admit that this passion was late in coming to you."

"When I started this destructive habit, it was not so much by passion, but to satisfy my Haitian pride. When I saw the latest American goon driving frenetically on the sacred earth of the fatherland, I told myself that I deserved contempt if I continued travelling by buggy or by foot. And notice that I'm a benevolent motorist, I let everyone enjoy my *hippogriff*, down to the last pedestrian—youngster, old lady or *gendarme*! People I pick up off the street, or my most fashionable friends! Lords or ladies! Whether they're coming home from funerals, weddings or the cinema."

"Oh! You know, when you die, you'll be deeply missed in Port-au-Prince!"

"That's for sure! . . . Where can I drop you off?"

"Outside my office."

And the Dodge set off.

THAT VERY AFTERNOON PABLO stopped by Mr. Brion's house. The latter greeted him cordially but did not ask him any questions—such was the lawyer's custom.

Nevertheless, the intelligent man's penetrating look embarrassed the Cuban, who began to blush.

"Listen, *Maître*," he said, "I cannot bear the thought that you think ill of me. The words I said here the other night were a gimmick, and I know well that you were not douped for a second. I was too ashamed to return here since then. But it was not a vile intention that made me act this way. I was forced into it by an irresistible sentiment called love, and I strove to gain the trust of the neighbour, since I am in love with his *señora*, madly in love! I hope you will forgive my childish little ruse and keep my secret. Love excouses all."

"That's not true!" Mr. Brion cried sharply. "Love does not excuse all! Where did you come up with such theories? They are antisocial. That woman is not available. You have no right to take her from her responsibilities."

"And if she loves me? And if she is unhappy with her husband?"

"If she loves you, it is your love that gave rise to hers, you are thus responsible for her troubles; and if she is un-happy with her husband, again it is your love that is the cause, since before she knew you, she lived quietly and contently, if not happily."

"Verily," exclaimed Pablo lyrically, "you speak of love as an ordinary thing! But it is the only reality that counts in this world and the only thing that brings happiness! And the human creature has a right to happiness, which is only possible through love! You were saying recently that your compatriots are enemies of liberty and truth. You could also add art to that list; and if they are, it is because they despise love. Love is the wellspring of liberty, truth and art—the love of a woman, the love of nature and the love of life!"

"You mustn't generalize like that," said Mr. Brion. "There are nations that have done great things, but for which love was of secondary importance—reason, ambition even, was the framework of their greatness."

"It is possible, I do not deny it, but I proclaim," Pablo went on, growing more and more impassioned, "that from the moment that two beings love each other, they belong to each other by right!"

"Fine," said Mr. Brion, "but when there is a husband between those two beings . . ."

"He only has to make himself loved, or defend what he sees as his possession, knife in hand! As for me," Pablo added, with evil eyes, "I am ready to challenge Céphise's husband for her in a closed arena, at knifepoint!"

Mr. Brion could not help but laugh at the idea of Mr. Hellénus Cato in a knife fight, in an enclosed space, against this madman, to keep his wife.

"You laugh," Pablo continued, still agitated, "I assure that this is no laughing matter. Where I come from, love and death go hand in hand. You know what happened to my friend Epitacio who was my roommate in Havana?"

"How could I know? I am not a wizard like your friend Manès."

"Well then, I will tell you. My friend Epitacio fell in love with a young woman who lived across the street from us. She was married, and every afternoon she would go out onto her balcony with her husband. Epitacio would go out onto his balcony and make eyes at her. This seemed to please the lady. One day, the husband noticed; he got up, went into his room, then came back armed with armed to the teeth. He emptied his weapon onto Epitacio, who fell down stone dead.”

“What savagery!”

“No!” yelled Pablo. “It was passion! The husband, by his energy and decisiveness, held onto a woman whom he loved and who maybe did not love him much, but who fell madly in love with him since he killed a man as not to lose her. People pitied Epitacio and approved of the husband, who was acquitted by the tribunal.”

“Here,” said Mr. Brion, “we have gentle manners. Love is calm. We seek and find happiness in marriage. Love quickly transforms into a pleasant duty, and our main concern is raising children, not looking out for idlers making eyes at our wives in order to empty rifles on them at point blank. Haitian women are, in general, honest, pleasant, devoted, and even when they don’t think their husbands deserve their tenderness, they don’t make a big deal of it. And scandals are rare. If your friend Epitacio had come to live in Haiti, he could have made eyes at all of the women, they would have smiled, and their husbands would have mocked him, but no one would have had the heart to kill him. He would have ended up marrying a young woman who would have given him lots of children, but, he’s dead, so . . .”

Mr. Brion’s humour won the Cuban over, and the latter said that he intended to marry the lady he loved.

"It's not the same thing. The woman that you love has a husband. You want to edify your own happiness over the pain of another, and that's evil."

"But," Pablo continued, "if the manners of your country are as gentle as you say, why would her husband not do for me what the other Cato—the Roman, Cato of *Outica*, who was a very transcendental man—did for a friend! Plutarch says that Cato of *Outica* gave up his wife Marcia to his friend Hortensius, who wanted her just like I want *Señora* Céphise. And I ask you to notice that Marcia was pregnant at the time that he gave her up to Hortensius —a state into which Cato of Haiti has never been able to put his *señora*!"

Mr. Brion laughed heartily at the comment.

"Yes, I know," he said. "And Cato of Utica even took Marcia back after the death of Hortensius. But we cannot permit ourselves the same fancies in our time. Even in antiquity people were stunned and shocked by Cato's act, even though they were used to the rigid stoic's eccentricities."

"So, I was only kidding when I spoke of Hortensius's sit*ou*ation," said Pablo.

"I wouldn't have thought otherwise," said Mr. Brion.

"But it is no joke," Pablo continued, "that I swear I will marry my lady after she has divorced, and I will go off with her and never leave her."

"You think that she will consent to divorce in order to marry you and immediately follow you abroad?"

"Yes, because she loves me."

"That is not a sufficient reason."

Pablo turned entirely red.

"Come on! You think that a woman whom you love and who loves you would refuse to free herself to marry the man she loves and run away with him!"

"You wouldn't think that if you understood Haitian women."

"Haitian women are monsters, then."

"On the contrary."

And Mr. Brion, not wanting to say that Haitian women dislike scandals—because he did not want to insult a guest—sought an explanation, and when he found it, he expressed himself thus:

"Haitian women are such that no consideration, sentimental or otherwise, will make them abandon the known for the unknown."

The handsome fellow smiled and, aware of his worth, said, "You will see that *Señora* Céphise will leave the known for the unknown."

"Then," said Mr. Brion, "that will be an exceptional case, and my observation will be no less true, in general."

Meanwhile, Mr. Brion had noticed that the whole afternoon, Céphise had not appeared in front of her gate. He thought that Pablo knew the reason, since the young man showed no sign of anxiety.

In any case, Pablo judged that he had spoken too much about his sentimental affairs, and he told himself that the moment had come to let Mr. Brion know about an opinion he had heard expressed about him, the night before, in a house where he had dinner and spent the evening playing games. This will amuse him, he thought, and when a gentleman goes to someone's house, he is expected to say all sorts of things that might amuse his host.

"I was somewhere last night, *Maître*, and they were saying good things about you."

Mr. Brion was perfectly unaffected by the good or bad things that might be said about him. He stayed silent.

"I had just got up from the gaming table at the Orcels' place . . ."

"Did you win?"

"Yes, as always," Pablo replied ingenuously, and added, "well, after the game, I started chatting with Madame Orcel who, from what I can tell, is a very distinguished woman. She asked me if I liked the country and if I had met any interesting people. I responded: 'Of all the people I have met, the one I have been most impressed by, after you Madame, is Mr. Brion, the lawyer.'

"'Yes,' she said, 'he's a very good man,' — 'Oh! Yes, Madame, he's a remarkable man, transcendental!'

"That was when she told me something that struck all the more vigorously because Madame Céphise had previously told me something similar. 'Mr. Brion,' she said, 'is the only man who knows how to talk to women in this country.'"

"Really!" Mr. Brion cried, "I wouldn't have expected that of her!"

"You like that, eh?"

"Not at all. I would rather have the gift of making them love me than just being able to talk to them—though I admit that I do have the latter gift."

Pablo closed his eyes and muttered:

"When you know how to talk to women, you hold the secret of making them love you."

"The secret to making women love you is being young, handsome and rich—and this third quality suffices most often."

"Ah! But you are bitter Mr. Brion."

"You think so? . . ."

At that moment, out of a buggy that had come up the road, a lady showed three-quarters of herself and turned her visage toward Mr. Brion's *galerie*. She must not have been able to discern very much, twilight already giving way to night. But Pablo recognized Céphise, who was returning home from the city where she had made a few purchases.

Nothing was keeping the Cuban at Mr. Brion's house. He got up, obsequiously said farewell, and left. He went quietly over to Mr. Hellénus Cato's house.

Passing by his Overland, he stopped and seemed to reflect for an instant, then he continued on without haste, leaving the car where it was, which is to say next to Mr. Brion's archway.

CHAPTER VI

PABLO HAD BARELY PASSED through the *porte-cochère* of Mr. Hellénus Cato's villa when he perceived a human form stirring in the shadow of the orange trees that lined the driveway. It was Céphise. She was waiting for him, there was no doubt. Yet she feigned a lively surprise.

"You frightened me!" she exclaimed.

He replied, not insincerely:

"It is you, rather, who frightened me."

She let out a choppy little laugh.

"Suppose," she said, "that we both were both frightened."

Then, he took the hand that she had abandoned to him and squeezed it passionately. From his lips, the words were flowing, disjointed but full of fire. he wanted her all to himself; he was ready to fight all the way to Hell for her; for her, he would kill anyone; and to keep her, he was resolved to walk in streams of blood. In the end, his utterances overflowed with all the passionate Spanish phraseology—taken by emotion, Pablo imbued his French with countless Spanish terms. He was all the more eloquent for it.

And since these excessive declarations always please women, even though they feign indifference, Céphise listened to Pablo in ecstasy—especially since he, talking all the while, covered the *bonita señora*'s face with passionate kisses.

But lovers have this in common with our friends the Americans: the more ground you give them, the more they want. Soon Pablo was no longer satisfied with her face and made it clear to Céphise that he wanted all of her. But the young woman resisted him and rushed to the villa where she found Mr. Hellénus Cato, who, under the right *galerie* where four electric lamps were liberally emitting light, was finishing the newspapers of the day—or of the evening to be exact. He seemed distressed.

He did not notice the emotion that so agitated his wife. To herself calm down, she began telling him all about her afternoon errands in the city. Mr. Hellénus Cato barely paid attention to this story. He was still under the shock of indignation that had seized him when he read that the President, in the course of the day, had gone sailing. He told his wife about this news, which he considered an outrage. Céphise, as not to contradict him, pretended to share the point of view of her husband, whose calm was restored by this approval.

"I am certain that the whole public thinks like us," said Mr. Hellénus Cato.

In fact, the whole public had thought like them. Nevertheless, the historical truth obliges us to admit that, on this serious affair, a certain number of moderate persons thought differently from Mr. and Mrs. Cato: they did not think that this cruise was an outrage, but they considered that, at least, it was 'tactless.'

Céphise was busy removing her hat, when Mr. Hellénus Cato got up abruptly from his chaise longue, and his face was illuminated as if a divine apparition had just appeared before him.

It was Pablo who had just revealed himself at the entrance to the *galerie*. Mr. Hellénus Cato went to meet him and took both his hands, which he shook forcefully for several seconds. When Pablo managed to disengage, he approached Mrs. Cato, to whom he presented his compliments. The Cuban's lips formed a smile, but his eyes, normally full of gentleness, expressed a cold hardness. Céphise understood; he was unhappy that she had abandoned him under the orange tree. She thought he was being inflexible, and, to show him she was angrier than he was, barely responded to his greeting. Pablo understood and gave in.

But Mr. Hellénus Cato found that his wife was undermining his interests by giving such a poor greeting to a man who, by his heavenly knowledge, could help him find a fortune and solve all of his problems. He promised himself he would set her straight as soon as he had the opportunity.

Since it was seven o'clock, Mr. Hellénus Cato asked Pablo to do him the honour of having soup with Madame Cato and himself.

The young Adonis accepted, and Céphise went off to give the order. After a few words about the weather, Mr. Cato, visibly distracted, asked Pablo to excuse him for a minute and he went to join Céphise in the office. He harshly scolded her for treating such a useful man so inconsiderately.

"He must be treated kindly, my dear, very kindly," insisted Mr. Cato, meaning no harm.

"Well then! Since you insist, I will be very kind to him," said Céphise, meaning no good. "But search me," she added, "I don't see what Mr. Alcantara can do for you."

"You don't see . . . With him, I will have everything."

"Everything?"

"Everything!" he said, with a large gesture that encompassed the world.

"Very well. I'll do what I can to make him happy."

And, quite satisfied, Mr. Hellénus Cato joined Pablo, under the right *galerie*, rubbing his hands together.

He resumed their conversation on the weather, which was very fine, and complained at the infrequency of rain, worrying about the fate of the upcoming harvest. Soon, Céphise came and sat in a rocking chair facing them, and agreed that the lack of rain was deplorable. Not for economic reasons, like her husband, but for domestic reasons; the lack of rain left families defenceless against the dust.

"I'm forced to wipe the furniture as many as six times a day, it's tedious," she moaned.

"Port-au-Prince is the only large city in the Antilles without a sprinkler service," said Pablo.

"It's shameful!" Mr. Hellénus Cato cried with humour. "These Americans don't do anything!"

On this last word, Bernadotte appeared, now in the role of butler, and murmured:

"Dinner is served!"

They headed into the dining room. The soup was consumed solemnly. What's more, it was excellent.

"More soup, Mr. Alcantara?"

"Please," said Pablo, who had regained his sweetness.

"And you, Hellénus?"

"Of course, to accompany our friend."

Pablo bowed politely, and at the same time, under the table, he slid his foot under that of Céphise.

Mr. Cato, at that moment, exposed the affair of the President's sea voyage and asked for Pablo's opinion on the matter. Pablo did not see anything wrong with it, but to please his host and indicate, at the same time, his respect for public opinion, he said that he, in fact, found this cruise to be a provocation.

"That's the opinion of all upright folks and others," said Mr. Cato.

Bernadotte presented a carved, roasted chicken. Pablo served himself a thigh and a piece of white meat. Mr. Cato, who was watching him anxiously, was satisfied to see that the young deity had disregarded the gizzard, which the patriot adored. He hastened to serve it to himself with a few more of his preferred pieces. Céphise made do with a piece of white. Usually, she focused on the giblets, which she held between her thumb and index, first shredding them energetically, but she could not allow herself such liberties in front of a foreigner. Pablo had good table manners. He only used his knife to cut the pieces he had on his plate; while our friend Hellénus used his for all sorts of purposes and dipped his bread audaciously in the sauce dish—and thought he was being proper.

The wine was a Graves, very dry and very respectable. Pablo hardly took a drop, to which he added a good deal of ice water.

Generally, a Cuban is sober.

While they ate slowly, the lovers' feet, under the table, were not idle. Céphise was wearing silk stockings, and Pablo wore socks of the same quality, held up with garters. And nothing is more pleasant that playing footsies in these conditions, or so say the enthusiasts. Céphise and her sweetheart experimented and decided that the enthusiasts had made a perfectly correct assessment.

Bernadotte, having changed the serviettes, served the macaroni, which the party devoured, and then arrived the dessert, which was quickly dealt with.

After the servant had finished serving, he withdrew.

Pablo lit a cigarette and Mr. Hellénus Cato, a cigar. Suddenly, the latter cried:

"Monsieur Alcantara, for days I have wanted to ask you a question and I have not dared until now . . ."

"But, my dear friend," said Pablo, "you offend me in speaking thus. I beg you not to be afraid to talk to me. Consider me as one of your own. Speak, I beg you, speak."

"Very well!" Mr. Hellénus Cato continued. "I would like to know if, based on calculations on the moon, one might find a hidden treasure."

"That depends on the available data," Pablo replied, annoyed.

And he explained that, for example, if someone possessed an authentic item relative to the existence of a treasure in a specific area, without knowing in which part of the area the treasure lay, then yes! By calculation, one would come to know with certainty exactly where to look.

"And . . . if we do not have an item?" Mr. Hellénus Cato asked uneasily. "If the only data we have is a hypothesis? Dreams?"

"Dreams?"

"I mean fancies. By calculations, could one come to determine where to look, in accordance with the general data from these fancies?"

The worried Cuban looked at Mr. Cato with haggard eyes, believing he was being mocked—and for the present, under the table, the game of footsies stopped.

But Mr. Hellénus Cato was not joking in the least. Never in the whole of his exemplary life had he been more serious. And he was afraid that a negative answer would follow. Which is why he felt he had to add the following explanation:

"You see," he said, "at the end of my property there are traces of a structure from the colonial times. It has always been believed that the colonist who lived on this land buried his fortune here, and more than twenty times I have dreamt that I succeeded in laying my hands on this treasure after a lucky dig. I have carried out attempts on the terrain, but without result. Is it possible that, with the calculations you told us about, one could know precisely the spot that holds this treasure?"

"We shall have to see," Pablo stammered, embarrassed.

"See what?"

"Well . . . my manuscripts . . . my notes . . . Manès's *Red Notebook* . . ."

"Can you not proceed like the illustrious Manès when he masterfully discovered the treasure of the Aztecs for Carranza?"

"But it is not the same thing. Manès, on that occasion, was working based on sec*ou*lar traditions, which had never varied, and not based on a fancy."

"Why not try?" said Mr. Cato who got up and went out to the *galerie*, where he started examining the moon, which was rising majestically in the sky.

At that point, Pablo, enveloping Céphise in a tender glance, rebuked her for having been so mean and cruel!

"It wouldn't have been prudent for me to stay in the driveway any longer," Céphise murmured, looking downward.

"Listen," said the other briskly, "I have rented a little house in an almost uninhabited neighbourhood, we could meet there . . ."

"Never!" Céphise exclaimed.

"Why?"

"Because all of Port-au-Prince would know about it within an hour and my reputation would be ruined for the rest of my days. Find something else."

"Find what?" Pablo moaned in despair, turning red like a rooster. "You will not go elsewhere, and he is always here! Not to mention the servants . . ."

"If you love me like you say you do," Céphise replied in a little tone of ferocious coquetry, which drove the Cuban crazy, "If you love me like you say you do, you will find something."

"Yes, I will find it," Pablo exhaled passionately, "I must find it!"

Mr. Hellénus Cato, after contemplating the moon, went into his office and returned to the dining room with a sheet of paper and a pencil.

"Eh? What must you find?" he asked, laughing heartily.

"The treasure!" Pablo replied assertively.

Mr. Hellénus Cato was thrilled by the response—and Céphise even more than him.

"Let's see now," said Mr. Cato, placing the sheet of paper and pencil in front of Pablo, "let's see now, begin!"

"Begin what?"

"The calculations to find the treasure, of course—the moon is in all its splendour."

"Oh! This is not how we must proceed . . . there are rituals . . ."

And at that moment, a glimmer crossed the Cuban's mind and he let out a resounding shout:

"Ah! That's it!"

"At last!" Mr. Hellénus Cato exclaimed raising his arms toward the ceiling in satisfaction, "this should be good!"

Pablo rose to his feet as if shot up by a spring. He went to get his hat, then came back and bowed to Céphise who offered him her hand.

But, in Pablo, the man of the world had disappeared to make room for the Mage.

"What, are you leaving?" Mr. Hellénus Cato asked, pale with astonishment.

"*Sí!*" said Pablo, who seemed to be sleepwalking.

"But . . . the calculations?" said Mr. Cato, pointing to the things he had put on the table.

"Not today."

"Why? The moon is there, three-quarters full, and waiting for us."

"Not today."

"Did you not just say: 'That's it!'?"

"I said it, it is true, but I shouldn't have."

"Listen, Pablo, you are discouraging me!" Mr. Hellénus Cato cried in an impassioned protestation.

After a moment during which Pablo seemed to intensely evoke who knows what, he spoke in a solemn tone:

"Well then! Tell me, are you resolved to do anything I tell you?"

"I will do anything you command," Mr. Hellénus Cato replied in an inflection of humble submission.

"Very well then. I must go and perform the necessary rituals immediately, as the great Manès indicated in the *Red Notebook . . .*"

"Tomorrow, then!"

"Tomorrow!"

And Pablo left mechanically, signalling with his hand for Mr. Cato not to follow him.

CHAPTER VII

PABLO'S ATTITUDE, WHICH HAD initially amused Céphise, began to worry her. She felt, from that moment, a hint of distrust for the handsome man. And then . . . she thought he was going too fast, being too hasty. Haitian women do not go for that type of thing. They are women for whom love develops slowly. It could take years before their loves are realized—or not. But like this, all at once . . . Ah! No! Céphise was terrified.

After Pablo left, she went up into her room, got undressed, carefully washed her face, donned a snow-laced bathrobe, then went out into the moon-soaked terrace where she stayed for some time, reflecting on her situation, feeling trapped, tangled in the mesh of a steel net and not knowing how to escape.

If at that moment, the young man appeared in front of her and took her in his arms, she knew she would put up no resistance because the physical attraction would be too strong. But then her sense of morality reared its head, and she promised to avoid being alone with him—which was easy.

Easy? or so I thought so, she responded to herself, when I asked him to find another way, I didn't think he would be able to come up with anything since it was impossible here and I refused to see him elsewhere. And then thanks to Hellénus's stupidity, he has outmanoeuvred. If only I was protected, but I'm not . . . on the contrary! And what's worse, I don't even know this man! And I let him do those things! . . . Well then! . . . Now, I have to buy time. That's the only way I can defend myself. Yes, I will defend myself!

She took a few steps, looking without seeing all the beauty that surrounded her: the sombre green of the glistening trees in the clear and cool night; and the facing mountain, which blocked the horizon, that pale blue mountain that stretched out sleepily in the moonlight, under the twinkling stars . . .

That's it, I will defend myself . . . but how? she though, desperately twisting her hands, because as soon as he touches me, I lose all my strength.

She turned back, slowly and silently heading toward the door that to her bedroom, then stopped as she was walking through it, reflecting deeply on the problem at hand. Suddenly, she swung her arms and cried:

"Ah! Zut!... I've had it! *M pa renmen anyen anbete m!*"[1]

---

[1] Haitian Creole in original. Translation: I don't like anything to bother me!

And with that, she went back into her room, took off her bathrobe and the rest, replaced them with a mauve lace nightshirt that was as short as a vest, then slid between the sheets. She fell asleep immediately and did not wake until morning.

As for Mr. Hellénus Cato, he was even more agitated than his wife, who, at least, had control of her thoughts and could get the better of her worries with a brief and energetic word: "Zut!" and thus conquer sleep. But Mr. Hellénus Cato was not a man who could achieve such heights. Pursued, haunted, obsessed by an idea that was summed up in one word: "Tomorrow!" He could do nothing but dwell on it and spent the whole night tossing and turning in his bed without being able to shake it. He barely slept an hour, and even that was tormented, troubled, halting sleep! Then, when he heard the neighbouring clock strike four, he sprang out of bed with the enthusiasm of a young man! After a few summary ablutions, he put on his shabby morning clothes, consisting of a jacket and blue-striped, canvas trousers, a pair of loafers, and his chequered cap that was so thick that it would have brought joy to a Russian in Russia but could not please a Haitian in the tropics. While getting dressed, he was no longer repeating "Tomorrow!" but: "Today! It's today! This evening!"—that was all that had changed—and he pledged right away to take a long walk, from the top of Lalue to Bois-Verna, Turgeau and through Peu-de-Chose.

Soon he was ready and went down to wake up the maid, so she could prepare his coffee. Waiting for her to serve him, he started pacing back and forth in the right *galerie*, thinking it would be today that his property's great secret would be revealed: "Today . . . Today!"

Suddenly, he stopped in his tracks, struck by a phenomenon that his eyes had just beheld: there was light in Mr. Brion's house!

"He must be sick," Mr. Cato said to himself, "because we've been neighbours for years and this is the first time I've ever seen his lights on at this hour. When I go out, in a few minutes, I must ask Napo for the news concerning Mr. Brion."

Mr. Cato, his mind thus occupied, had ceased to be pressed by the obsession that had bothered him since the night before. The state of anxiety verging on lethargy gave way to the disposition of a normal soul, which gave his nerves a relative rest.

Meanwhile, he was served a cup of coffee which he drank in small sips. After that, he lit a cigar, then, grabbing his *cocomacaque*, he went out into the driveway.

As he neared the exit, he noticed that Mr. Brion's house was no longer lit up and he saw Mr. Brion himself quietly walking up the avenue—which isn't really an avenue because it isn't lined with trees—not seemingly in a hurry.

"He's not sick then," Mr. Cato said to himself, "and he doesn't have the pace of someone out for a walk. Where is he going like that? Back when we were masters in our own house, I would have thought Mr. Brion was involved in a political conspiracy. But now . . ."

As he made these reflections, he followed Mr. Brion twenty paces behind, though he had no real intention of tracking his noble friend. Still, he followed him absent-mindedly, mechanically, pulled along by the movement of the man ahead of him, for whatever reason. But truth be told, Mr. Brion was being followed by Mr. Hellénus Cato. So much so that Mr. Cato, who was guided more by Mr. Brion's light palm-beach suit than by the pale and inter-mittent electric lights, soon lost sight of the man, as he had descended into the Louis Roy-Dupuy Lane. Then Mr. Hellénus Cato rushed to reach the aforementioned lane where he arrived out of breath just in time to see the clear form immediately drown in the morning mist. Mr. Cato started running again and did not slow down until he saw that the form he was following had just disappeared into Bois-Verna Avenue—another avenue that isn't lined with trees, and consequently isn't one—and then reached it himself. But there he did not see anything in either direc-tion.

"Blast!" Mr. Cato cried, "I've lost his trail."

And so, with no compass but his sleuth's instinct, he quickly went back up the avenue. The daylight was already beginning to show itself in its crude pallor. Passing the little road that is home to our friend Pradel's mansion, Mr. Cato took a glance and saw Mr. Brion who was still wandering, hat in hand. Mr. Brion crossed the bridge, passed by the Saint-Louis Chapel on his left, and headed toward Turgeau—another non-avenue avenue—which he descended slowly. Mr. Cato slowed his pace and continued following him. Arriving outside Sacré-Cœur,

Mr. Brion stopped, apparently unsure whether to continue to the left or the right. The orb of the sun was starting to rise behind the Bourdon hills. If he were to go left it would take him down Peu-de-Chose with the sun on his back. Mr. Brion decided not to spoil his little jog, and continued to the right, heading home by the other section of Turgeau and the Chemin des Dalles.

Mr. Hellénus Cato thus understood that Mr. Brion had simply taken a little walk, which was his right, and the patriot blushed for his shameful espionage, though he did not regret it—because as he returned home, with a majestic gait, he found he was cured of the obsession that had tormented him since the night before.

Arriving home, Mr. Hellénus Cato made a copious meal of a ham omelette and a steak, then reclined in his chaise longue, after furnishing himself with Vacherot's book on democracy, and slept until noon when he had to be woken up for lunch. Again, he did his duty, his full duty! After that, he went back to sleep, still with Vacherot as a soporific, and woke up around four o'clock. Then, he took a bath, and got ready to go over to Mr. Brion's house, where the 'audience' would bring him to seven o'clock, at which point Pablo would arrive to do the calculations that would give him a treasure—to get started . . .

CHAPTER VIII

"I SWEAR TO YOU, THEY'RE leaving!"

"And I repeat, they won't go."

"Who's that?" asked Mr. Delhi, who had just arrived in the driveway, with the intention of taking Mr. Brion to Pétionville.

"We're talking about the Americans of the Occupation—the 'marines' as they're called," replied Mr. Renaudin.

"And where are they going?"

"To their filthy and prejudiced country, which they should never have left," said Mr. Hellénus Cato with disdain.

"Well then! To hell with them! I applaud them frenetically!" exclaimed Mr. Delhi, shaking the hands of his friends who were seated under Mr. Brion's *galerie*. After that, he threw himself onto a chaise longue and thought for a few seconds. Then, regaining his sangfroid, he added:

"By the by, what are you basing your assertion on, Hellénus?"

"On what everyone is saying . . . and on something inside of me, that screams they are leaving."

"I see that your sources of information are nonexistent," said Mr. Delhi. "I thought you had received secrets from your friend Russell."

"Monsieur Russell is not my friend," belched Mr. Hellénus Cato, offended.

"Fine . . . fine . . . don't get upset, you puritan, we're kidding, that's all."

"I don't suffer jokes," said Mr. Cato, "when it concerns the liberation of my country!"

"Of our country, Hellénus, say of our country," Mr. Delhi suggested softly.

"I'm sorry," said Mr. Cato, still stern, "it was a *lapsus*."

" . . .*linguae*," added Mr. Delhi.

"Exactly . . . *linguae*. It wasn't a *lapsus calami*, eh?"

"Hellénus, how versed you are in Latin! It's striking!

'. . . It's striking!
Like water blindly shaken from a wet dog.'

to use the illustrative language of Victor Hugo, or as a Haitian poet described it, in an unforgettable sonnet:

I melt away . . .
And my untamed body carries on in one plane.

And all this to translate the succinct French expression: 'I've gone baba.' Isn't poetry wonderful!"

"I wouldn't want to contradict the literary appraisal you've just delivered," said Mr. Brion, "but it seems to me that the exact interpretation of the latter verse that you cited should be: *m rete rèd!*"[2]

"I don't deny it," replied Mr. Delhi, in the serious tone he could assume when talking about silly things, "but you'll allow me to point out that you raise a question of aesthetics that could be discussed for hours. Go into any city in France and yell: "I've gone baba!" Everyone will understand you, and after that yell: *m rete rèd!* and no one will know what you're talking about."

"Without a doubt," said Mr. Brion. "My interpretation only concerns the Haitian poet's verse."

"And the even more vulgar French expression, it refers to the French poet's verse?"

"Exactly."

"Then you believe that the Haitian verse, that has every appearance of a French verse, is, in the end, nothing but the translation of a thought in Creole?"

"But . . . certainly."

"And so, when Anténor Firmin wrote: 'I held a butterfly,' and Demesvar Delorme retorted, 'he translated *kenbe*,'[3] Delorme was right (because you don't hold a butterfly, you catch it). And the example of the Haitian verse in the French style being the translation of a thought 'in Creole' is the same as Firmin's phrase that was rectified by Delorme?"

"Yes . . ."

"That's all I wanted to hear," said Mr. Delhi, "and I ask your forgiveness for stringing you along by the Socratic

---

[2] *m rete rèd* = I stopped dead (Haitian Creole)
[3] *kenbe* = to grasp (Haitian Creole)

method. Villevaleix couldn't come to terms with our expression "*flanke yon kal*,"[4] which is as pithy as anything, and is easily as expressive as the French "*rosser d'importance*," or "significant thrashing" that the author of Primèveres gave as an equivalent to the Haitian expression."

"And your conclusion?"

"Is that, because of our context, the French that we speak and write is no more the French of France than the English of the United States is that of the British—and I might add that nothing is more ridiculous than a Haitian purist . . . But, Hellénus, what's the matter? Is it because, by chance, literature also horrifies you?"

"My dear Mr. Delhi," replied Mr. Cato, "you are an enigma to me." Mr. Cato pronounced the word 'egnima.' "We have the same political opinions; like me, you are a rabid anti-Americanist, and like me, a die-hard patriot! However, as soon as we meet up, you start to make fun of me. It's rather rude if you don't mind my saying so."

Mr. Delhi stood and retorted:

"My dear Hellénus, I beg you to take this advice: this country has no more honour, no more public life, no more commerce, no more memories, no more literature, no more mirth. All has gone dark in the face of the American! But there's one thing that the American will never be able to destroy: Gérard Delhi's good humour! And when the Grand Soir comes—and I hope to be there when it erupts into flames!—I'll howl with laughter as, under Dessalines's invocation, I shatter those stranglers of the lower class, those destroyers of weak nations, with rifle shot!"

---

[4] *flanke yon kal* = give a beating (Haitian Creole)

"Bravo, Delhi!" Messrs. Renaudin and Hellénus Cato exclaimed.

"Naturally, you don't think like me, you rational man," Mr. Delhi said to Mr. Brion.

"You're ranting," replied the latter, shrugging his shoulders, "and the saddest part is that you're listening to yourself."

"Oh! I see what you're playing at," said Mr. Delhi sitting back in his chaise longue, "but I warn you that I won't let you turn me into an object of ridicule."

"I wouldn't dare, old friend, I'll leave that up to you," said Mr. Brion.

"You think I'm wrong then? Aren't we in a humiliating situation?"

"An occupied country is always in a humiliating situation."

Mr. Delhi lit a cigarette and seemed to think for a moment, then he began talking, as if to himself.

"All told," he said, "our situation before the Occupation wasn't so bad. We did some stupid things, to be sure, the regime was a mess—remember, Hellénus, how terrible you were to me when you opposed me, along with the other cabinet members, to force me out of the Ministry because I was against a printing project intended to pay off fictitious debts!"

"They've done better since then!" said Mr. Renaudin. "What could be more fictitious than Monsieur James P. MacDonald's debt! His contract? Inexistent! His railroad? A joke! MacDonald himself, isn't he an imaginary being? Who has ever seen MacDonald?"

"Yes," Mr. Delhi resumed, "it was a bit mixed up. There was violence, a few cynical robberies, fanciful printing of paper money, customs racketeering, frauds in the public works that required a comparative study, the purchase of a warship when the books said they had built a school; frauds on supplies, and on ordering, ordinances, and on rationing and balances and other childishness; when it went too far, we'd have a little revolution, some wealthy people would go into exile and others would replace them and have their turn for fun. Obviously, there was the matter of the shootings, which is nothing to laugh about. A word from our old Plésance will happily qualify the state of things: "Our country's history is a bloody operetta!" Admittedly, all that was absurd, but it was bearable."

"That regime was abhorrent," said Mr. Brion, "because it was against liberty."

"Be that as it may! The Americans came, and what did they do? Did they help us get on the right path? To make our institutions operate sincerely?"

"Yes, the regime of the Simulacra . . ."

"Exactly. That, however, was the weak point of the Haitian system that had to be straightened out. Not only did they do nothing about it, they ruined everything, creating a reprehensible regime—for them as much as for us—which cynically prevents control by qualified, legitimate political bodies, just as the pure Haitian regime had hypocritically done."

Mr. Brion retorted:

"But they gave us the regime you're asking for! In 1917 there was an elected Chamber and Senate (you were even part of one of these assemblies). But with this detachment from reality and the taste of the Simulacra that characterizes the Haitian mentality, the Chambers began to protest and refused to adapt our institutions to the Convention. The Americans acted logically; they decided the only thing to do with such people was to send them packing and set up a system that you call reprehensible, but a system that was amenable to their business interests, since that's partly why they are here, to do business. The United States is more of an economic than a political entity. I think that when they have achieved their aims they'll give us back our representative regime, and then we can protest to our heart's content."

"But by then the country will be tied up like a sausage!" exclaimed Mr. Renaudin.

"What a lovely refrain of moans and groans!" said Mr. Brion. "Ah!" he added, "eloquence is alive and well in Haiti."

Mr. Delhi had taken an ironic and cheerful attitude as if Mr. Brion's reasoning was only worthy of his disdain.

He abandoned the main question and attacked his opponent about a detail that he considered weak.

"You dare to maintain," he said, "that the United States is more an economic than a political entity. Well, that's heresy! It might have been true in the time of our professor Boutmy at the École des Science Politiques, but it has ceased to be the case for the last twenty years as that country has constantly meddled in other countries' affairs, to the point that the next global coalition will be against them!"

"You're right," said Mr. Brion, "I should have said that the United States is as much an economic as a political entity. The immense country is bursting with so much wealth that today they have considerable interests everywhere and there is spread across the whole planet—and consequently they must have a political dimension."

"So," resumed Mr. Delhi, "they're not only here bothering Haiti for economic reasons, but also, and particularly, for political reasons, if they're really coveting Port-au-Prince as a naval base."

"Incidentally, did you hear anything about the naval base question?" asked Mr. Brion.

"Nothing," Mr. Delhi replied. "But it had 'leaked,' just like everything 'leaks' in our country. An American friend of mine implied that they won't start thinking about the base until next year."

"Ah!" said Mr. Brion, "so you have a friend among the Americans."

"Certainly," replied Mr. Delhi, "and everyone knows that, as a lawyer, I have quite a few American clients, and my clients are necessarily my friends. Besides, I berate them often enough, and they find it natural that we're offended when their government mocks us. And in all honesty, I can't deny that, for their part, they're upset with the biased decisions that some of the judges of our tribunals make against them."

"You said it!" said Mr. Brion.

"A judge should be above all those contingencies," Mr. Delhi continued. "His role is to judge according to the law, no matter whom he is judging; it should not matter if he's a patriot or not. A judge is a judge, that's all. Unfortunately, that isn't always the case."

"Ah! I couldn't have said it better!"

No one replied to Mr. Brion's exclamation, and Mr. Ranaudin broke his silence to bring the conversation back to the original point.

"Getting back to the naval base," he said, "it seems to me that last year's Washington Conference limited naval armaments; a treaty to this effect was even signed in December 1921 between England, the United States, France and Japan, in the hopes of a general peace."

"That's true," Mr. Delhi responded, "but it didn't prevent England from pursuing the execution of a major project regarding the naval base in Singapore, along the most direct route leading to India and Japan."

"That only concerns the Pacific," said Mr. Renaudin.

"But the United States borders the Pacific as much as the Atlantic," Mr. Delhi replied.

"I read in *Le Temps* of Paris," said Mr. Brion, "a political report on the matter, and even the British Admiralty is suggesting that the Singapore Naval Base should be large enough for the entire English fleet to dock there, and the House of Commons has just approved ten million pounds sterling for the project."

Mr. Hellénus Cato, for a long while, had regained his anxiety, and seemed absent, lost in his thoughts. However, at this point, he shrugged his shoulders and grumbled:

"It doesn't concern us."

"Possibly. It's still worth mentioning," Mr. Brion continued, "that the English want to have a fleet that is capable of travelling as a whole on any ocean and of destroying any enemy, and for that, they must construct bases, without which the whole system is condemned to failure. The report from *Le Temps* is clear about that. Under these conditions, the United States is obligated to have a policy to match the strong British notion.

"Do you still think that it doesn't concern us, and that it only matters for the Pacific, which, since the Panama Canal, is no longer isolated from the Atlantic?"

"Surely the Americans will harass us on the matter!" Mr. Renaudin moaned.

"The opportunity is too good for them not to take advantage of it!" said Mr. Cato, who had pulled himself together some.

"I don't think they'd establish a base in order to harass us, but strictly for defence," said Mr. Brion.

Mr. Delhi smiled and, with satisfaction, watched the swirl of his cigarette smoke rising to the ceiling.

"What are you thinking?" Mr. Brion asked.

"I'm thinking about the next war," Mr. Delhi responded, "and the *kal* that the allied fleet will *flanke* on the American fleet right in our vicinity. I'm looking forward to it! And then, old chap, what better chance to trigger the Grand Soir!"

"You're playing with fire," said Mr. Brion. "It's perfectly possible that the American fleet will defeat the allied fleet —and therefore because our situation means we're expected to help our Great Friends however we can, a part of that victory will rebound to us. What a day for Haiti!"

"You are endlessly irritating!" Mr. Delhi exclaimed. "You take satanic pleasure in contradicting your friends in the way they see things, and you enjoy tearing apart their dreams. It's obnoxious!"

"The wise must always consider the pros as well as the cons," said Mr. Brion, laughing.

"Well then! Can I just say," Mr. Delhi exclaimed, "you are corrosive!"

"Oh!" said Mr. Brion, "That's what Victor Hugo said about Voltaire: 'Voltaire is corrosive, Mirabeau is a sledgehammer!' It's meaningless."

Mr. Hellénus Cato, who had seen a car pull into his driveway, got up to leave. He shook Mr. Brion's hand limply, and those of Messrs. Delhi and Renaudin energetically.

Mr. Renaudin smiled sweetly as he watched Mr. Cato disappear into the evening.

"Let's say, by some chance, the Grand Soir erupted in Haiti, Hellénus would quietly stay home sick . . ."

"As for me," Mr. Delhi exclaimed fiercely, "you'd see me in the streets, you know full well!"

"And me too," cried Mr. Renaudin.

"Yes," said Mr. Brion, still in the same tone, "I know; you, Renaudin, to preach pacification and humanity to the fanatics; and you, Delhi, to rescue as many Americans as possible!"

Mr. Delhi, who was kindness itself, couldn't stop himself from laughing:

"You're right," he said, "I'll rescue each and every one of them with my steering wheel. It's stronger than me!"

"In that case, what would become of the Grand Soir?" said Mr. Brion.

Mr. Delhi, exasperated, cried:

"You disgust me! You're simply corrosive!"

And then, calming himself, he added:

"Let's go! Let's head to Pétionville! My old Belle-Brune has prepared a little meal for us, and that's all I'm saying! Renaudin, come with us!"

Mr. Renaudin was about to leave, his hat on his head.

"It's impossible," he replied, with a bitter sadness, "I have a wife and kids; I can't run around wherever I please like you who have no responsibilities in life!"

"Thanks!" said Mr. Delhi. "Meanwhile, we envy you! You've got if figured out!"

And as Mr. Renaudin went to find Mr. Brion—who was busy closing all the doors with infinite care—to shake his hand, Mr. Delhi rushed up to Mr. Renaudin and said:

"No, Renaudin, I'm taking you with us in the car and we'll hand deliver you to Madame Renaudin whom, I haven't seen in a while, and I'd be happy to pay her my respects."

And speaking thus, he led Mr. Renaudin toward the exit. Suddenly, he stopped; and as if having a grave error to remedy, he exclaimed:

"And Moustapha?"

He was Renaudin's second son. He was actually named Jules, but Mr. Delhi had given him the nickname Moustapha because of the child's Carthaginian complexion, and his big puffy face.

"Jules is doing well," replied Mr. Renaudin, who did not want the nickname to stick to his son, whose ugliness and heaviness of spirit were already troubling enough.

"Ah! That Moustapha!" continued Mr. Delhi, "I adore the boy! Hey, I should give him a bicycle, as a gift!"

"No, no!" yelled Mr. Renaudin, terrified, "there's no need! It'll be a source of trouble for our home . . . No, no, if you please, Delhi, no bicycle for Jules!"

"A little hunting rifle, that would be great for Moustapha, eh?"

Mr. Renaudin went pale and responded:

"Even worse!"

And he added:

"Nothing. You shouldn't give Jules anything."

"Okay, fine, I won't give anything to that brave Moustapha. For now!"

Mr. Brion, having finished closing all the doors and windows of his house, now gave instructions to his devoted servant, the famous Napo, former police commissioner under the old regime. Napo lived in a little room in the courtyard that almost connected to his boss's office.

The instructions consisted of surveillance checks that Napo was to carry out every two hours, throughout the house, during the night, to prevent robberies.

He feared for his books—which were all he loved in the world—as if nocturnal robbers ever took books!

And then he put on his hat, lit a cigar, and joined his friends who were waiting for him in the car. Napo brought him out his travel bag, which contained everything necessary for a man ready to leave for New York, even though he was just going to Pétionville for one night.

And as the car set off, he cried:

"Napo, keep watch!"

CHAPTER IX

PABLO FOUND CÉPHISE IN THE large west-facing *galerie*. She was standing near a pedestal table, rifling through the fashion magazine *La Femme Chic*, with her back to the entrance. She had taken this position as soon as she heard the car pull up in front of the steps.

The sound of Pablo's footsteps in the *galerie* made her turn around.

"Ah! *Bonsoir*," she said.

He bowed to her and covered her hand with kisses.

When he straightened up, he complimented her on the clothes she was wearing, which were delectable.

"I have never seen you so pretty," he said, as if in ecstasy.

"You don't look so bad yourself this evening," she replied cheerfully.

The young man was wearing a tussar suit, and his eyes and his hair gleamed with lively radiance.

However, he said:

"I would have preferred to find you undressed."

"Well, I never! How dare you!"

He did not have time to respond. Mr. Hellénus Cato, back from Mr. Brion's, was in the *galerie*. He rushed up to Pablo and took his two hands:

"My friend, my excellent friend, since last night, I've hardly lived, I've waited so anxiously for the moment of our Pythian task. Are we starting right away?"

The Cuban assumed a mysterious bearing:

"We can start the task," he said, "around ten o'clock, when your servant and the neighbours are asleep."

"Ah!" said Hellénus, heartbroken.

"I am sorry. But it will not be possible before that time."

"Then we will have dinner," said Mr. Cato.

Pablo accentuated his mysterious attitude:

"You cannot have dinner; all you are permitted is a bit of soup."

"Very well, I'll only have a bit of soup."

"Good."

They went to the table. The soup was served, and Mr. Hellénus Cato ate slowly.

"My dear friend," he said, "you can't imagine how much I would like to meet Manès."

"Ah! He has a hard time travelling."

"I know. He only works for kings and heads of state."

"But if the price is right, he will work for anyone."

"You think so?"

"I am sure of it."

Mr. Hellénus Cato began daydreaming and finished his soup in absolute silence.

In the meantime, a little drama took place under the table. Pablo's feet did everything in their power to find those of Céphise, and were unsuccessful. The handsome man tenderly sought an explanation and a bit of pity with his eyes, but Céphise responded with a look of innocence.

Pablo only felt more amorous.

Mr. Hellénus Cato, condemned not to eat, had crossed his arms, giving no notice to the words exchanged by Pablo and Céphise, which seemed trivial to him: they spoke of love and polished off the remaining courses with the strong appetites of youth.

Pablo told the story of his friend Epitacio, saying that, in his country, love is a very serious matter, and elopements were very common, and it was a pity that it was not the same in Haiti.

Here, Mr. Hellénus Cato, following up an idea that had absorbed him, asked:

"What colour is he?"

"Who?"

"Manès."

"Oh! Well, you know, he is white."

"How old?"

"Sixty-five."

"Does he have a beard? I picture him with a beard."

"Oh! *Sì*, a big beard."

"Black?"

"Indeed, black."

"Large?"

"Well, he is as big and as corpulent as you!"

"Really!"

Mr. Hellénus Cato was greatly flattered to have the corpulence and the size of an extraordinary man like Manès.

"Is he married?"

"Indeed."

"How many children does he have?"

"Twelve."

"He's a patriarch, then?" said Céphise.

"You said it, Madame, and when I said he has twelve children, I should specify that they are all of the masculine sex."

"That's wonderful! And all from the same mother?"

"Exactly! Manès is a saint: he has never known a woman besides Tété."

"What a strange name!" Céphise exclaimed, laughing.

"In Cuba, every lady named Térésa, young or old, is called Tété. It is a nickname."

"Ah! Very good," said Céphise. "And even better, he has set a great example by staying with one woman his whole life."

"Yes, he's a great example," said Mr. Hellénus Cato sombrely.

"Unquestionably."

Speaking this way, they had arrived at dessert, which they took care of in less than five minutes.

Pablo lit a cigarette and offered a cigar to Manès's admirer.

"I'm allowed to smoke?" asked Hellénus cautiously.

"Yes," said Pablo, "but just one cigar—not two!"

"Thank you."

And thus reassured, Mr. Hellénus Cato lit his Havana with calmness in his soul.

Then they moved into the salon. Céphise sat at the piano and played "Mon Homme," but much too fast. Pablo, who was a bit moved, slowly executed two or three Cuban *danzóns*, which entertained his hosts.

Soon it was nine thirty.

"We can begin," said Mr. Cato, "all the servants have gone to bed, and there are no lights on in the neighbours' houses."

"I am at your command," said Pablo, who pulled a little red notebook out of his pocket and consulted it with fixed concentration. Céphise glanced at the pages.

"What strange writing!" she exclaimed.

"They are hieroglyphics," said Pablo casually.

And he passed the item to Céphise's husband.

Mr. Hellénus Cato flipped through the notebook with reverence, then he carefully returned it to its owner; and since he did not understand anything, he was struck with profound admiration.

Pablo, now, was standing in the opening between the salon and the dining room. Suddenly, he shouted:

"Madam Cato must quietly retire to her room and go to sleep immediately! I wish her a good night! Mr. Cato can follow her and must immediately come back down with a bath towel!"

The couple took to the stairway and disappeared. A moment later, Mr. Hellénus Cato reappeared with a bath towel draped over his arm.

"Close all the doors and windows, except for the ones in the salon!" Pablo commanded.

The master of the house obeyed.

"Turn out all the lights, except in the salon, where you will only leave the *bombilla* near the piano!"

"B*ombilla?* . . ." Mr. Cato asked timidly.

"The bulb, of course!"

"Ah! Very good . . ."

And Mr. Hellénus Cato flipped off all of the switches on the main floor, except for the one controlling the bulb near the piano. Then he went back over to the boss, waiting for the final orders.

"Now, go p*o*urify yourself!"

"How do I 'purify' myself?"

"Right, go bathe yourself in your big basin! You do not have to stay in the water for more than one minute!"

Mr. Hellénus Cato bowed, went out the left door of the salon, crossed the *galerie* and the garden, arrived at the basin room, undressed, and then plunged himself into the water—all this, at ten o'clock on a chilly April night.

In the meantime, Mr. Pablo Alcantara carried out an inspection—he hurried up the stairs; arriving on the top floor, he sought and found Céphise's room; he spoke briefly with the young woman, then he left her. He rejoined Mr. Hellénus Cato at the moment the latter came out of the bath.

"Wipe yourself off quickly," he said, passing him the towel.

Mr. Cato obeyed and began to redress.

"No!" said the other. "The ritual is not valid unless you stay in the state of nat*our*! Come!"

They left the basin room; Pablo closed the door and put the key in his pocket—locking up all of the personal effects of Manès's admirer.

The night was clear, calm and cool. In the pearly sky, the moon beamed in all its milky splendour.

"You will go to the middle of the garden," said Pablo, "where you will stay, observing the star god until I call you."

"What am I looking for?"

"You are looking for everything you see. If, for example, clouds hide the celestial body for a moment, you have to take note of it, and count how many times the phenomenon takes place. In the end, you must remember everything that crosses your mind about the god of the night."

"I have no prayers to utter?"

"No, I am the one who will utter the prayers, in the salon where I will stay. I have to say each of the seven incantations in Manès's red notebook one hundred times."

"How long will the ceremony last?"

"An hour . . . An hour and a half at most."

"Very well."

And as the neophyte went to take his designated place among the flowers, Mr. Alcantara made a smooth gesture:

"Wait," he said. "I must not be able to see you during the ritual, and neither can anyone else. You will begin as soon as you see me go into the salon and close the door leading to the *galerie*. Go on then, see you soon, and be strong!"

"Count on me!"

The Cuban did as he said, except after closing the door to the *galerie*, instead of starting to spout Manès's supposed incantations, he went up and found Céphise, with whom he spent an unforgettable hour in the warm and perfumed bed. All the while, Mr. Hellénus Cato, bronze antique that he was, stood naked in the middle of the garden that cold and silvery night, obstinately contemplating the moon . . .

Sustained by faith, the patient man undertook his appointed task resolutely. When, after an hour and a half, his deliverance arrived, he remained unwavering in his attitude of a god scoffing at the elements.

At the appointed time, the door that led from the salon to the *galerie* opened and a voice cried:

"Monsieur Cato, go under the canopy of the basin room, and I will join you there right away."

The bronze statue began to move and slowly made his way to the indicated spot. Almost at the same time, Mr. Pablo Alcantara arrived nearby. He opened the door and, pointing to the clothes scattered on a bench, he said:

"Get dressed quickly, Monsieur Cato, you must be cold."

"A bit," said the other.

"Did it go well?"

"Excellently. I saw extraordinary things."

"I am not surprised. But you will tell me about it later. All the same, I must warn you that Madame Cato cannot know what has taken place."

"That goes without saying. A ritual is a ritual."

"That is right. Are you ready?"

"Yes."

"Let us go inside then."

When they entered the house, Pablo turned on the lights, then personally opened the door to the dining room. Mr. Cato went over to the stairway and wanted to call to his wife. But Pablo stopped him.

"Let her sleep," he said.

And opening the kitchen cabinet, he took everything he needed and began to make a hot American grog for his friend, his great friend. Mr. Hellénus Cato swallowed the grog as quickly as he could and felt rejuvenated.

"You know that now . . . you can eat," said Pablo tenderly.

"Thank you, my friend, thank you . . . I am, in fact, quite hungry."

Pablo took some cold roast beef out of the pantry, set a place at the table, and served his great friend with touching devotion.

"And you, Pablo, aren't you going to have anything?" asked Mr. Hellénus Cato with a critical look.

"Yes," the other replied, "I am going to have a glass of white wine after you have had one."

Pablo poured a glass of Graves for his great friend and then served himself.

"How friendly you are! To your health, Pablo!"

"And to yours, my great friend! And to the achievement of your most intimate desires!"

"Thank you, Pablo, thank you!"

Mr. Hellénus Cato, having recovered, gave a long sigh.

"A cigar?" said Pablo.

"With pleasure."

"It is getting late," Pablo resumed, pulling a notepad out of his pocket, "please give me the results of your observations."

"Very well!" Mr. Cato responded, "I noticed that the clouds went in front of the moon four times while I was in the garden."

Pablo wrote: 'N°1— 4 times clouds on moon,' then he stopped:

"Thick or thin, the clouds, the four times?"

"Thin."

He added 'thin' then closed the notepad and put it back in his pocket.

"And the extraordinary things you mentioned?"

"I meant 'an extraordinary thing.' One is enough."

"What was it?"

"Well! My friend, I saw Manès himself, just as you described him to me, between the moon and myself, just as I see you right now, across this table."

The Cuban could not prevent himself from smiling.

"Good, good," he said.

"You're not going to note this phenomenon?"

Pablo touched his forehead with his index finger:

"Yes," he said, "I will bear it in mind."

"What are you waiting for to start the calculations?"

"But we have not finished! The experiences, in the present case, have to happen seven times! It is on the total of the observations multiplied by seven that we will or will not obtain the favourable results that we are searching for. But, so far we only have one seance to draw from."

"So, I have to go through tonight's ordeal six more times?"

"Precisely. I should point out that while you are going through a bit of an ordeal, I am working too, you must not forget that."

"I didn't forget it. It's just that I had thought—wrongly, I realize—that a single seance would do the job."

"The end will justify the means."

"Oh! I'm not arguing. And as someone else said, I'm in it until the end!"

"Me too!"

Then, Mr. Pablo Alcantara vigorously shook Mr. Hellénus Cato's hand, and then took leave of him, wishing him a good night.

"See you tomorrow, Pablo!" was Mr. Cato's only response.

CHAPTER X

THE SIX NIGHTS THAT FOLLOWED Mr. Cato's first ordeal went by in similar fashion. After the seventh ordeal, Pablo did his calculation, which gave no result, as one could guess. He declared that he did not understand, and Mr. Hellénus Cato was struck with bleak despair.

"Ah! If only Manès were here, he'd find it."

"That's for certain."

"Quite certain."

And now the poor man's mind was wracked by the thought that he must have Manès come to Port-au-Prince —Manès who did not really exist, Manès who was nothing more than Pablo's invention. But he needed Manès, and he was ready to make sacrifices in order to meet the illustrious friend of heads of state from faraway places.

He ended up asking Pablo the question.

"Do you think the great Manès would consent to travel for a thousand or two thousand dollars?"

"No less than five thousand," replied the other, who could see good things coming his way.

"Damn!"

And the unfortunate man fell into a profound meditation.

Meanwhile, strange rumours were starting to make their way through the neighbourhood. Chérilus, the Ancelin family's coachman, in hesitant tones, spoke of having seen Mr. Hellénus Cato doing 'babooneries' at night, naked as all get-out, among the trees of his garden—while a little foreigner was shut up with Madame in the house.

The Ancelins lived to the left of the Cato household.

But the neighbours to the right, the Jean-Bart ladies, respectable people with whom Céphise went to the cinema every Sunday, declared that these words were slander; that if all that were true, they would have known about it. And since they had not seen anything of the sort, it must be false. The Jean-Bart ladies had, for a long time, considered themselves the moral police, not only of the neighbourhood but of the city. When they defended the honour of a compromised lady or an imprudent young woman, this had a certain significance, because immediately, two parties would form: one for, the other against, and finally, the accused ended up benefiting from a generally favourable uncertainty. That's what happened for Céphise who was given the benefit of the doubt, having found in Mr. Brion a defender who was as unexpected as he was mysteriously disinterested.

When Napo came to report Chérilus's claim to Mr. Brion, the latter, along with the data he already had, did not doubt their truth for a second; however, he replied:

"Such nonsense shouldn't be repeated, Mr. Hellénus Cato would never act like such a 'baboonist' and his wife is honest; Chérilus was quite certainly drunk when he saw the villainous things he's reporting."

Napo took him at his word. After that, he did not fail to treat Chérilus as a drunkard each time, in his presence, the coachman started talking about what he saw.

The Jean-Bart ladies did not fail to tell Céphise about the rumours that were floating around about her and about how they had defended her—and they warned her to take every precaution against the little Spaniard whom no one could trust.

The fact was that Céphise was even becoming suspicious of Pablo—which is the inevitable fate of all schemers: the numerous and mysterious tête-à-têtes that the Cuban was having with Hellénus; his elusive attitude toward her. And then there was what she had seen! She had seen, during the last late-night ordeal, right when Pablo had left her, she had seen, through the *jalousie* of her bedroom, Hellénus stark naked in the middle of the garden, and she had grasped with horror and with pity how much Pablo had made an ass of her husband, whom she was attached to, despite everything. She had gotten ahold of herself from that moment, and from then she had rebuked all of the Cuban's propositions—he now seemed diabolical to her.

Then, she began to see her recent conduct as despicable. The smallest sound made her tremble. She feared everything, so tormented was she by remorse. She prayed.

She had been a woman of faith, but she was distraught and weak to the point that prayer, which wards off misfortune, so they say, did her immense good. The image of He who is all goodness, all forgiveness, and all mercy penetrated her soul. She went to confession and then received the Holy Communion.

And so, she found peace of heart and gained the strength necessary to resist temptation . . .

MR. BRION KNEW THAT PABLO had two passports, one in his name and the other in a false woman's name, and was planning to leave, without warning, for Santiago de Cuba, by the steam of the Empresa Naviera. He knew, in addition, that Mr. Hellénus Cato had mortgaged one of his great storehouses at Bord-de-Mer, for a value of five thousand dollars. Hellénus being practically bewitched by the Cuban, Mr. Brion had no doubt that the money was destined to go to the latter, who was going to carry out the unbelievable blow of running away with Mrs. Cato and having the costs paid by the husband himself!

Mr. Brion was sure that the Cuban would not leave without coming to bid him farewell, and he was waiting for that moment to expose the Cuban's latest plan. Preparing for every contingency, he kept Napo at the ready, after having prepared him for the role he had planned for him to play.

One afternoon, Mr. Brion was standing in his library flipping through his Tacitus, when he saw Pablo, suitcase in hand, coming up his driveway. Immediately, he called Mr. Delhi on the telephone and asked him to come pick him up with his car, but not to come up the driveway, but just to honk the horn. Then he went and opened the door for the Cuban, who was knocking on the door to the salon. Mr. Brion responded coldly to his greeting and asked him why he was visiting. The character was pale, and his hands were quivering, but without letting go of the suitcase, which Mr. Brion guessed contained Hellénus's five thousand dollars.

"I have come to bid you adieu," said Pablo, "I am leaving momentarily, and before I embark I wanted to give you my regards, and to express my thanks for welcoming me into your home."

"I don't believe," Mr. Brion replied in a glacial tone, without offering him a seat, "I don't believe you should give me your regards nor your thanks, given your conduct toward my neighbours across the road, my friends, which was so dastardly."

"I acted for love," he said, lowering his head, "as you know well, even if others do not. I made the woman love me and I have her in my blood; she gave me her latest favours and after I had prepared everything, I asked her to leave with me. Not only did she categorically refuse to follow me, but she added that she had never loved me, and that, if at any moment she had forgotten herself, it was because of my sorcery! When I heard that I saw red, and I wanted to kill her. She realized this and said with calm resolve: 'I will never be yours again, even if you kill me, as I see the desire to do so in your eyes; but it is finished, finished, finished between us.' Then I felt that I loved her more than ever. I was annihilated. Ah! You know your compatriots well!"

"And now, what are you going to do?" asked Mr. Brion, who seemed not to notice the last exclamation, which he considered a compliment.

"Well!" Pablo replied in a decided tone, "I shall take her all the same. I must have the last word!"

"You want to abduct someone who doesn't consent?"

"Yes. She will come back to me. I sense that she is currently under the power of someone else's will, some priest no doubt!"

"Where is her husband?"

"I sent him to Léogâne for an observation."

"Lunar?"

"No, he's examining a tree. He will not be back until this evening. By then we will already be halfway through the Panama Canal. I will leave him a word about Mrs. Cato's absence. He will think his wife is in the mountains of Arcahaie for two weeks—in keeping with orders from Manès."

"Why do you use your amazing intelligence and energy to do evil? With such gifts, on the right path, you could have achieved a high post, I'm telling you!"

"It is for love . . ."

"No. Because you've also stolen five thousand dollars from Hellénus, which is pure knavery."

Pablo grew even paler and stammered:

"It is still for love, nonetheless . . ."

Mr. Brion did not press the point and seemed to be thinking about another matter. He knew that trying to trick Pablo was a losing battle, so he continued his systematic domination on the basis of fair play.

"Listen," he said suddenly, "I don't see how you can abduct a woman without her consent."

"With chloroform, it is easy," replied the self-satisfied young man, "and I have already arranged the embarkation, which will be child's play."

"You're forgetting something," Mr. Brion said calmly but firmly. "I won't allow it."

Pablo was distraught in the face of this determined man whom he had believed was detached from everything and incapable of action, due to his egotism and love of tranquility.

At that moment, a car honked in front of the fence; that's Delhi, Mr. Brion thought, all is going well.

"But," Pablo began to sputter, "what do you care if I take this woman who is nothing to you and whom I love with all of my being?"

"I care," replied Mr. Brion, "because I have no problem with defending her individual liberty. It is a duty of conscience for me to save that poor vulnerable woman, who was so happy with her life, and who single-handedly enlivened this sad neighbourhood with her laugh and her bearing."

"What do you mean, save her?"

"Yes, I want to save her, because I know what she's getting into. Because I've seen them, abroad, the poor little Haitian girls, supposedly freed, having left with handsome young men of your type. They become managers of gambling dens or prostitution houses if they don't sell their bodies to feed themselves and their boyfriends. So, knowing this, I decided that I had to prevent the crime that you are planning to commit."

"Listen," said the scoundrel with a homicidal look in his eyes, "listen . . ."

Mr. Brion interrupted him dryly:

"No. Enough! You will leave here and embark this hour, otherwise I will denounce you to the *gendarmerie*, by telephone, as a con man and a seducer."

Pablo, pallid, sweating profusely, retrieved the suitcase which he had set on a chair near where he was standing.

"Useless," he said, "I will embark. It is all my fault, I never should have trusted you."

"Insolent! So, you thought I would be your accomplice!"

Pablo, in his sly little manner, made like he was leaving when, on Mr. Brion's signal, he stopped, and did a three-quarter turn toward the exit.

"I'm warning you," Mr. Brion cried. "I'm going to have you followed and you'll be under my surveillance until the boat leaves; and on the first sign that you're trying anything at all, I'll have you *fouke*."

"*Fouke?*"

"It's a Creole expression from the time of our greatness. It means: arrested and put in jail."

"I am at your mercy and I recognize that you are sparing me much," said Pablo. "I promise you I will forget the abduction, but as for the other matter . . ." and he stared at the suitcase.

"Oh!" said Mr. Brion with a thin smile, "it would be improper of me to get mixed up in an affair of interest that my friend Hellénus had entrusted to you. I would only have dealt with it if you had forced me to. Since you promise to be reasonable, I only have one last thing to say to you: *bon voyage!*"

The scoundrel smiled, bowed respectfully, and left.

As soon as he had turned his back, Mr. Brion called Napo and completed the instructions he had already given on the subject of surveillance to implement on the Cuban, adding, "Telephone me immediately if you notice the slightest questionable thing in his actions."

Napo grabbed his *cocomacaque*, and Mr. Brion led him to Mr. Delhi, telling the latter to follow Pablo's car, which had just set off, and to drop Napo off at the port.

"Honestly!" Mr. Delhi cried, upset, "you asked me to come here in my Dodge to drive your servant to the port. Ah! No, gentlemen, you're really abusing my kindness this time . . ."

"Idiot!" said Mr. Brion tenderly. "Just know that you're helping to save a woman who, if not for us, would have been lost forever. I'll tell you the story on Sunday, in Pétionville. Now, go. You're going to lose that miscreant's car if you don't leave this second."

Mr. Delhi started his engine and drove off with Napo who, as a former police commissioner, hoped that affair would end to his satisfaction, which is to say the circumstances would give him the opportunity to administer a masterful thrashing to Pablo—a matter of 'getting his hands dirty' in the process of doing good.

After the car had gone, Mr. Brion went back into his house, straight into his office, and positioned himself to monitor all comings and goings at the Cato residence, then he resumed reading Tacitus as if nothing had happened.

Around seven o'clock, Napo returned and gave his report. The Cuban had gone directly to the port, brought his car to the individual who had purchased it, and then boarded the boat, not moving from the deck until the anchor was raised. Only then did he seem calm.

"And how do you know, Monsieur Napo, that the Cuban had sold his car?"

Napo explained that it was consequent to the intervention of Mr. Delhi, who had insisted on knowing the details of the sale. He nearly even had business with the Cuban himself, but Pablo managed to avoid it.

"Is Mr. Delhi coming here this evening?"

Napo replied that he was not; that Mr. Delhi had gone to have dinner at Sea Side Inn with many of his friends; that tomorrow morning all his time was taken up by a literary contest for young girls, since he was a member of the jury; that tomorrow afternoon he was busy with a tennis match at Marian and tomorrow evening it was his turn to attend the chess party at the Ortels' place.

My poor Delhi, Mr. Brion thought, how he torments himself to avoid boredom! The car isn't even enough!

"So," he said out loud, "he didn't tell you when he's coming by here?"

Napo explained that Mr. Delhi would come pick up Mr. Brion on Saturday evening and take him to Pétionville.

"Very good, Napo, you've done a fine job! The five gourdes, and the five cigars on the table are yours as well. Take them and go in peace!"

Right when Napo left, the maid came to announce that dinner was served.

Mr. Brion headed into the dining room and ate lightly, such as it must be in a hot country.

He no longer thought about that afternoon's incident. His reading of Tacitus had transported him far into the past. He had a vision of the Roman Republic, which was so great and strong and magnificent. Then his mind was filled with the other Rome, the Empire depicted so bleakly by Tacitus, and yet which is unforgettable. And he wondered into what miry sea a great people who have lost their liberty can be driven . . .

CHAPTER XI

THE DANGER GONE, CÉPHISE regained her good humour and her carefree attitude, or rather her seemingly carefree attitude, since her recent experience had affected her character in some way.

She now had a way of boldly looking men in the eye, as if to defy them.

The religious practices that had helped her get through the crisis that had so tormented her became a show as soon as the crisis had passed, since her faith was not the sincere, profound, alive faith of true believers, but a small spasmodic faith that could spring to life and then disappear with the calm.

Not having children to care for, nor religious faith to sustain her, and having lost her companion—Hellénus had lost his senses—she fell into an intense ennui.

The comings and goings in the road, which had once amused her so much, now just seemed erratic, and the cinema, which before then had interested her above all else, now bored her to tears.

Love can withstand hate but not distrust—and it was the latter that killed the passion she had felt for the scoundrel. The individual she had loved was so dead to her that it was as if he had never existed; the woman's ability to forget was so limitless once she had stopped loving. But Céphise had remained receptive, which is to say her heart was abounding with love, a love without object; she felt a great need for tenderness and she grasped at ghosts. Then those ghosts took on a human form. She wanted to love a good, strong and honest man whom she could be proud of and could trust. She cast her devotion on Mr. Brion, the man who was the master of her heart. She believed she could conquer him easily and allowed herself some foolish audacity. One evening, while walking along the road, she dared to go into his house, teasing him, and, under the pretext of entertaining him, she kissed him right on the mouth. He talked rationally to her, and since he had a burning fear of public opinion, he recommended that she not give rise to slander by suspicious conduct, and that, given the tendency of people to sniff around others' private lives, he asked her not to come back to his house.

She opened her eyes wide:

"Honestly! You're afraid of being judged?"

"Not exactly. I'm thinking about you."

"I don't care what people say about me!"

"You should. You should set a good example."

And she candidly burst out laughing:

"You know, some people think you're mad, and I've always defended you, but I'm starting to think they're not totally wrong."

"They say that, do they?"

"Yes."

"And you believe them?"

"Firmly."

"Indeed, I am a madman. Not two months ago, when I stopped that little Cuban from his plan of chloroforming you to abduct you, and I sent him away alone on the double!—Was that really the act of a rational man? What was I getting mixed up in? What did it have to do with me?"

She got to her feet, very emotional, with tears in her eyes:

"So! It was you who saved me!"

"Madman that I am."

"I felt hunted, exposed to imminent danger, lost, and then suddenly, I felt I was protected, preserved, saved . . . I believed that it was God . . ."

"It was Him! I was nothing but his humble instrument."

"And it was you!... Then I am more than nothing to you?"

"No one is nothing to me."

"Then you love me a little?"

"I have goodwill toward you."

She pouted:

"Oh! Goodwill . . ."

"Yes, goodwill, which is much better, rarer and more durable than love."

She came and sat near him, on the couch, and laid her head on his shoulder.

"Oh!" she said, "I'm thirsty for tenderness, for caresses . . ."

"You read too many romantic novels and contemporary plays. You speak like a heroine from Bernstein and from Henry Bataille. You must stop."

"I believe, indeed, that I've read them with too much passion. I won't do it anymore. You must tell me what I must do."

"Yes. Read English novels. They're healthy, honest and interesting if nothing else."

She sighed:

"Fine, I'll read English novels. I'll do anything you tell me to do. We'll become great friends. Except you'll have to come see me often. How hard is that? You just have to cross the road."

"I'll come see you."

"Often?"

"We'll see."

And saying these last words, he got to his feet and added:

"Now, go home."

She got up and said: "You're right, I'm off. Good evening and thank you!"

As she offered him her hand, he bowed and kissed it with obvious and tender respect.

Then, she left.

After that, she was no longer bored, so occupied was she with attempts to conquer Lionel Brion's inaccessible heart—and taking care of her husband.

MR. HELLÉNUS CATO HAD become like a body without a soul. Shortly after Don Pablo Alcantara y Toro's departure, doubt had set into the patriot's soul following a very un-orthodox word spoken at Mr. Brion's house, to the effect that Manès never existed outside of Pablo's imagination. The next day, Mr. Hellénus Cato returned to the lawyer's house and asked for the truth, the whole truth and nothing but the truth!

Mr. Brion declared that Pablo had admitted that Manès had never existed, and that, personally, he had guessed from the very beginning that Manès was a bait and switch.

"I swear," said Mr. Cato, "I don't understand why that boy told us all the lies that you're talking about."

"That boy knew the power of the Simulacra over souls without guiding principles and which are devoid of morals. And then, his plan was rather complicated; it involved invention, a storyline and other nonsense. I've seen the Americans string along the Haitian Government with simpler and more psychological methods—with a single word, a single syllable used ingenuously. Here, we're getting near the triumph of the Simulacrum! Ah! The Orientals have a great understanding of the souls of 'those who only care about themselves,' as Dante put it, and their 'open sesame' is profoundly symbolic."

"Yes," said Mr. Cato, "that's all well and good, but it doesn't explain Mr. Alcantara's actions."

"Ah! Now we're falling from the heights of psychology to the depths of roguery. But, my friend, Pablo's actions are simple. He caught you in a trap to steal your money—and other things, quite possibly."

Mr. Hellénus Cato went pale and protested with a pitiful audacity.

"That's not true, I didn't fall in the trap he set for me—if there was a trap!—Not a centime, you hear me, he didn't get a centime from me!"

"And I congratulate you, my dear Hellénus."

"And you, *Maître*, did you escape his talons unscathed?"

"Oh!" Mr. Brion laughed. "I wasn't as lucky as you. He only nicked . . . five thousand dollars from me!"

Mr. Cato understood the irony and bit his lip. He soon left Mr. Brion and went to the telegraph office of the Haitian consulate to Santiago de Cuba to ask for the news about Mr. Pablo Alcantara. He got the response twenty-four hours later: he learned that Pablo had left for Spain the same day he had arrived in Santiago, on board a Spanish transatlantic.

From that moment, Mr. Hellénus Cato was weighed down by a profound sadness. He no longer cared about anything, did not speak, hardly ate a thing!

He spent his days in a chaise longue, smoking an endless stream of cigars.

Céphise tried everything to snap him out of his depressing thoughts, to cheer him up; she was wasting her time.

The subject that, until that point, had energized his life —the government, its actions, its non-actions—now left him indifferent.

Mr. Brion, Mr. Delhi, Mr. Renaudin paid him a visit. He responded to these gentlemen's words with monosyllables.

Later, Mr. Brion returned alone, chatting with Céphise in Mr. Cato's presence; but the latter took no part in the conversation, though he seemed to follow it.

He had grown incredibly thin, only consuming eggs and milk. The doctors tried various treatments, not succeeding in improving his general state. He was more and more depressed. They tried to bring him back with electric shocks, and they injected him with Quinton serum. He felt a bit better physically, but his spirit was still suffering.

Finally, a trip to France was prescribed. Céphise gladly welcomed the idea, and Mr. Brion said the trip was as necessary for Céphise as it was for Mr. Cato.

Mr. Cato, when consulted, did not say yes or no. It made no difference to him.

Nothing made a difference to him now—and it was clear that he was in a state of general paralysis.

One month later, the Hellénus Cato household left for France.

CHAPTER XII

ALL SOCIETIES THAT FALL prey to the Simulacra necessarily begin to decompose and die before long, since they do not have the life-giving armour of liberty.

The people in the Orient who do not hold this principle are not living, they are simply existing.

Nothing can be established on Lies and Insincerity.

The Americans gave us peace and order, but the Simulacra, which were displaced by their mere presence, were re-established by them. The gifts they brought us were in vain, and all their work is like a dead weight.

Order and peace?

As Carlyle said—and it cannot be said any better:

"A brutal lethargy is peaceful; the fetid tomb is peaceful. We hope for a living peace, not a dead peace!"

And a living peace is only possible with freedom in all its forms!

In short, all we have before us is the Simulacra, and it is only a matter of preparing ourselves to make them withdraw and disappear—and to stop being Simulacra ourselves.

Haitian mothers, the fate of the Fatherland is in your hands!

Raise your children with the firm foundation of education: may they know how to obey and learn never to lie!

So, we will have women of Cornelian virtues and men capable of discipline, honour and virile patriotism!

And we will be respected—because we will be enriched by moral qualities, which have always commanded respect since the world began!

Let's roll up our sleeves, let's work! Push our sons toward the heights of Science and may Chemistry in her practical applications not be a secret to them!

The only great nations are those who respect the rights of others! In Antiquity, all the colossal dominators crumbled because their power was established on Injustice.

Just recently, we saw Imperial Germany and Tsarist Russia collapse because they believed that Force was everything!

The United States, if they must continue their vulpine policies against small nations; if they must continue playing the role of Regenerators of the Simulacra and the Chaperones of Corruption, they too will crumble—since Liberty is a Goddess who always takes her revenge on Swindlers, Liars and Pretenders who present themselves as Civilizers but are really Exploiters of the Weak!

And the United States will have ceased to be worthy of the great souls of Washington and Lincoln!

Haitian Mothers, cultivate your children in the indicated manner, and the Fatherland will not perish! The glorious day will come! The white Simulacra, just like the black

Simulacra and the yellow Simulacra will dissipate; and we will remain the masters of our forefathers' Heritage, thanks to the new virtues, the science and the courage you will have instilled in your sons—who will no longer need anyone for the development of their country by Liberty, Work, the Sciences and the Arts!

THE END

Acknowledgements

I would like to express my sincere gratitude to those who aided in the production of this work, in particular, Dawn Cornelio, Frenand Léger, Ian Shaw and Elaine Kennedy.